GW00503539

F.Z.CARSON

The Incident

By F.Z.Carson

F.Z.CARSON

The Incident

For my Mum with
my love always

F.Z.CARSON

Contents

F.Z.CARSON

Before the Incident

Humans are naturally creatures of habit. They will walk the same paths, eat in the same places, and wave at the same people every single day. They will cross at the same point in the road on their journeys and throw their empty coffee cup in the same rubbish bin on their way to work. These mundane practices make up the fabric of our lives; they are what make us human and what offers us balance, comfort, and stability. But to other people, these habits make us vulnerable, predictable, they make us easy victims. To these people, the watchers, the waiters, and the hunters, this is what makes us prey.

The Husband

The husband rolled over in bed and smashed a heavy hand across the top of his alarm clock. Immediately, the bone-jarring noise stopped, leaving only a memory ringing in his ears and giving him a chance to gather his senses. He opened his bleary eyes, rubbed the last evidence of sleep from them, and surveyed his wife. The alarm didn't wake her anymore; the loud, chaotic mess of chimes that started his day no longer bothered his wife. She slept through it. She lay as she always did, on her stomach, head turned to one side, last night's messy bun dishevelled and flopped all over the pillow, half contained, half wandering free, stray hairs spilling from it like jellyfish tentacles just waiting for him to get entangled.

He wondered if her hair could suffocate him and if he would awaken one morning to find a silky plait wrapped around his neck like a hangman's noose. Men always said that women with long hair were more attractive, but no one ever spoke of the dangers of sleeping next to such a creature.

Next, he examined the room; his clothes, neatly ironed and folded, ready for him to don before work, were waiting on the dresser. His keys and wallet lay next to them, parallel to the edge of the wooden unit. Precise and uniform. There was also a watch, not a regular watch but a fancy designer piece that could go into depths of four hundred metres and kept impeccable time due to its Swiss heritage. The husband hoped that it showed his status, what kind of man he was, and his place in the world. He needed people to know that he was superior, grander, and more refined. He craved their admiration and respect.

This side of the room was controlled. There was a place for everything, and everything was in its place. His wife's side, on the other hand, was a mess. Lipstick and perfume bottles were splayed across the sides, and there was a streak of foundation on the mirror and a dusting of powder across the wooden surface of the dressing table, like a morning's frost on a path. Clothes were spilling from the wardrobe like the tail feathers of an exotic bird, and odd socks were bunched up on the floor. Her jewellery box was open. Cheap costume jewellery spilled out of the sides; charity shop finds and family heirlooms that were most likely fake were mixed together, tangled like a nest of snakes.

He had given her jewellery. A beautiful gold pendant inlaid with diamonds and a watch, the feminine twin of his own, but they lay unused in their original boxes. His wife said they were too nice for day-to-day wear, and he didn't mind; she was always putting things down, and he knew she'd lose them. She lost everything.

How he hated this mess, the chaotic nature of his wife's side of the room in contrast with his order. Oddly, the same woman who could not contain her own possessions was a master at containing his. The shirts he wore to work were always ironed to crispness by her, the black shoes he knew were waiting at the bottom of the stairs were shined once a week by her, and the lunch box in the fridge would have been packed with her loving hands.

He had to admit that she was good at shining his shoes. She claimed her grandfather had taught her how to do it properly; it had been a throwback from his army days. She heated the polish and buffed them to a high shine. Afterwards, the shoes were always perfect, but his wife's face and hands would be streaked black with polish, grimy residue under her fingernails like a fungus.

God, how he hated her. He removed himself from the bed, taking no care to be quiet. Why should he try? He knew nothing would stir her anyway. He turned on the main bedroom light, and she buried her face deeper into the pillow, still not waking. Habit had forced his morning routine into the back of her subconscious. Instead, she carried on dreaming, imagining worlds of wonder that neither of them could touch in reality.

He walked into the bathroom and surveyed his face in the mirror. He had been told at some point he would have to shave every day, but it hadn't happened yet, so he shaved every two days instead: Mondays, Wednesdays, and Fridays. On the weekends, he left the stubble to grow unevenly across his face. He hated the stubble. Most men his age seemed to be able to grow swarthy beards worthy of pirates and kings, but his was uneven and pale and looked like a ridiculous peach fuzz after more than a day's growth. A teenager's facial hair was not fitting for the masculine aura he liked to portray.

He went through the same morning routine that he always did, with a military precision that came from years of control rather than a life in service. When he picked up his lunch from the fridge, it would be the same sandwich, bag of crisps, and chocolate bar that he had every day. He wanted something different, something bigger. But at the same time, he enjoyed the familiarity of the patterns he had adopted. If he had secrets, they would be well hidden behind the bland backdrop of his day-to-day life.

F.Z.CARSON

The Son

The son lay patiently in bed, waiting for his Mummy's alarm, snuggled under a cartoon duvet. He always woke up early; the sun light glinted through the curtains and cast dancing beams across his teddy bears, like the outside world was inviting him to come and join them. He surveyed the small clock on his bedside table and knew that Mummy's alarm would go off in five minutes, and they'd have to get ready for school. He would have a wash, brush his teeth, and put on his uniform while Mummy got ready. Some children in his class were still dressed by their parents, but he took pride in his independence. He was a big boy.

Then every day, like clockwork, they would meet at the top of the stairs, and Mummy would check if he'd done his teeth properly, tuck in his polo top, and tell him he was a very smart little boy and that she loved him very much. Mummy was free with her love; it flowed from her like the huge rivers his teacher had shown him in the picture books at school.

After, they would go downstairs, and Mummy would make him toast for his breakfast. He briefly wondered if today was Friday. On Fridays, he got to have chocolate spread on his toast as a treat. While eating his toast, he would take the opportunity to survey what Mummy was wearing. Other mums at his school wore jeans and jumpers and big coats with fur hoods, the kind of clothes he saw at the supermarket during the weekly shop. But his mum was different. She was a riot of colour in dresses and bright tights, with hand-knitted hats in the winter and big sunglasses in the summer. In his head, he loved how Mummy dressed. It made her different and fun, like the people on the TV shows he was allowed to watch after school if he was good.

But he also knew it wasn't normal. He'd seen Daniel's mum whispering about it behind her hand in the playground, and Emma in his class had come up to him one playtime and told him "Your mummy dresses weird". But he didn't mind; Mummy was Mummy. She didn't mean to make people stare, but she did. She liked colour, and it always made her easy to spot.

Once Daddy had let go of his hand at the zoo to answer his phone, he turned his back and began to walk off. For a moment, the small boy had been caught up in the chaos of the prams and grown-ups looking at the monkeys, the crying children demanding ice cream, and the gasps of the crowd as one of the animals had made a magnificent jump from one branch to another.

All alone, his small hands had started sweating, and his breathing had become shallow and uneven. But then he had seen a swirl of bright colour that could only have belonged to one person, the one person he needed and he was safe again. Mummy had swept him up in her arms, lifting him above the chaos and held onto him tightly. Later that night, when he was lying in bed, he heard Mummy shouting at Daddy for losing him. She was asking him with sharp jabbing words: What had been more important, the person who was on the phone or the safety of their son?

As soon as he finished his breakfast, they started the walk to school. The son liked this part of the day best; he had his mum's undivided attention. No phone to answer, no cleaning to be done, no Daddy demanding drinks or asking why the beds weren't made. They would chat as they walked, and sometimes she sang. Poems about two dead men getting up to fight, songs that she had heard when she was a small child living with his grandparents and knew by heart. He still found it hard to believe that his grandmother was a mummy; she was far too old. He wondered if Mummy and Grandma had walked to school hand in hand, singing songs. He'd have to ask.

He knew the route to school as well as she did. They always walked the same way, crossed roads in the same places, and took the same short cut through the back of town. This was his favourite part of their morning walk. The gritty stone path was hidden away by houses and had trees on either side. Great towering things that Mummy said were hundreds of years old. The son didn't understand the trees; how could something so old look new? Grandma was old, and she looked old. The trees were different. They looked fresh and shiny, not like grandma's soft, velvety face that was riddled with the lines and valleys of her life.

He loved the trees; they dripped water in the winter and provided cool shade in the summer. It was a magical woodland just off the beaten track, and he liked to pretend that he and Mummy were explorers and that only they knew about this secret path. That they had discovered it.

In reality, they weren't. He knew that from the other people who crossed their paths every day, the man in the suit and tie who would smile at them both but never offered a further greeting and the dog walker with the big, scary dog.

The Incident

The son hated dogs, especially that dog. It was large and black and barked and growled, spoiling the serenity of the secret path.

The Man in the Suit

The man in the suit smiled at the mother and her child. He never offered anything else, no word of greeting or spark of conversation. Years of bad relationships had left him distrustful of women, especially pretty ones. Now he only regarded them as objects of desire, suitable for one-night stands and nothing more. The woman herself was desirable, a wild sort of beauty with curves and loose hair. But he had noted her wedding band and the child who clutched her hand the first morning they walked to school. He considered them both complications his life did not need. So, he regarded her as off limits and kept his interaction to a minimum.

The Dog Walker

The dog walker stopped and tried to hush his noisy animal. He hated to see the child who also walked the path flinch whenever he noticed her, shrinking every time she barked and silently shaking as he passed her on the path. Bella, or Bella Boops, as he liked to call her, was a pain whenever she saw anyone, barking and jumping and generally making a show of herself.

Really, she was a big softy who would never hurt a fly, but her appearance and exuberant nature made her look like a threat. She was the breed of dog that is often seen on the six o'clock news, guilty of ripping off a small child's face or chewing the leg off a kindly old lady. She was the type of dog that made people alter their paths and cross to the other side of the street. She was the type of dog people signed internet petitions against and added to the list of dangerous dogs. The type people judged on sight.

But he loved her; for him, she was calm and lovely; for others, she was a terror. A walking nightmare in a fur coat. "CAN SOMEONE SHUT THAT FUCKING DOG UP?" A loud, angry yell came from one of the terraces that backed onto the trees. The dog walker let out a heavy sigh and tried to silence the dog, but it was useless; nothing would silence her now that she'd had a reaction. Bella, the big, exuberant dog, had taken someone else's moment of anger as a personal request for her to get louder and to have a conversation; now she was jumping, trying to get away from the heavy leash he carried in his hand. She wanted to meet the new friend who had spoken to her. This was the only place he could walk her without people informing him his dog was a danger, without having to endure the looks of strangers who made assumptions about his own character based on the dog he owned.

Yes, the child with his mother looked scared, but the mother herself seemed unbothered by Bella's furious displays. In fact, the dog walker often saw her as she walked home from school. She never made a move to touch the dog or stroke its smooth head, something that would have actually helped with Bella's outbursts. Attention was a surefire way of silencing her. But she always shouted good morning and smiled when it set Bella off barking.

The Owners of the Terrace

"Just close the fucking window" his wife muttered sleepily from beneath the duvet. Reluctantly, the owner of the terrace that backed onto the woodland path got out of his warm bed and closed the window. His body ached from the physical labour of the night before. He'd have to keep it shut from now on to drown out the noise of that bloody dog. Five mornings in a row, he had been rudely awakened by its loud barking. Normally he kept the window open, but his shifts had changed, and now he was working nights at the factory. His wife, who was a nurse, worked odd hours anyway. She needed all the sleep she could get so she wouldn't accidentally administer the wrong pills to a patient. She held life in her hands on a daily basis, and being well rested was sometimes the only thing that stopped her from accidentally letting it slip through her fingers.

He checked the clock on his bedside table and mentally calculated how many hours of sleep he could get before his next shift. His wife was already gently snoring; a long night as an A&E nurse had left her exhausted, both physically and mentally. Quietly, he wondered to himself if there was something he could do about the dog, not something cruel, but something to stop the noise. Maybe he could ask the walker to go elsewhere or persuade him to muzzle the animal. Could a muzzle even begin to silence the noise the dog created? He liked to sleep with the window open, and normally the path was quiet apart from the wind in the trees, the twitter of the birds, and on some mornings when you could hear singing. One morning, a quick glance out of the window, through the trees, led him to the conclusion that it was a mother singing to her child as they walked to school.

Sometimes, if he couldn't sleep, he would try and decipher the faint words; he recognised the seventies rock that his own father had played on an ancient record player. He fondly remembered his father placing the needle lightly on top of the shiny black vinyl, laughing as he dragged his mother away from a bubbling sink full of washing up and danced with her across the threadbare carpet, soap suds dripping from their entwined hands. Happy memories from a glorious childhood. He'd miss the singing now that the window was to stay closed.

The Son

The big dog was getting louder. He could see it just at the end of the path, a few feet from where they would cut through the trees. It was jumping now, its eyes rolling into the back of its head and drool pooling around his big, sharp teeth. The son shuddered for a moment and slowed his walk. "Come on pumpkin" he heard Mummy say. She was looking down on him, smiling.

He loved Mummy's smile. Some people he had noticed only smiled with their mouths. Mrs. Winwick, his reception teacher, was a mouth smiler. A big, cheesy grin would stretch across her face as she asked them in a sing-song voice to put away their pencils and sit quietly on the carpet. She had even had a mouth smile when she'd calmly explained to Daniel that he shouldn't wee in the pot plant in the corner of the room. Especially because it was artificial. The son wasn't sure what artificial meant, but when he told the pot plant story to Mummy, she smiled with her mouth and her eyes.

Her eyes twinkled when she smiled, and sometimes they twinkled when she wasn't smiling, as if she were trying to keep the smile hidden, but it was escaping out of her eyes, unbridled and determined to be seen. She had smiled with her eyes when Daddy had fallen over in the mud on holiday. Daddy had been very angry and, for some reason, had blamed Mummy for packing the wrong shoes. The son couldn't understand why Daddy was angry about his shoes. Mummy had packed every-body's shoes; in fact, they were all wearing wellington boots, which the son loved because it meant no pesky shoelaces and his were perfectly fine. He hadn't fallen over, and neither had Mummy; only Daddy had fallen over. Daddy, the son had noticed, only smiled with his mouth.

The Teacher

The teacher stood by the window of the classroom and watched as streams of children flooded into the playground. In her hand, she held one of her many "world's best teacher" mugs filled to the brim with stale staffroom coffee. Receiving a plethora of "world's best teacher" mugs was an occupational hazard when you worked in education, and even though it was very kind of the parents to even think of buying her a gift, she sometimes wished they'd just get her some decent coffee instead of the swill the school provided. Well, provided in the sense that every week she had to donate a pound towards the piggy bank and an extra fifty pence if she decided she wanted sugar.

She'd have to finish her coffee before the children came in, and she was greeted with her morning chorus of small voices. The head teacher's new rule was that no hot beverages were to be consumed in the classrooms while the children were there. Health and safety gone mad!

The teacher sighed. She was 65 years old and tired. Her bones creaked and ached as she crouched on the carpet next to small children who smelled of poo and play dough. Her mind felt soggy after years of explaining phonics to parents who "had been taught the proper way", as she tried to convince them that it was important to read with their children and that playing on a tablet was not as educational as they might assume, even if the game did say it would make their children the next Einstein.

As a young woman, teaching children at the start of their school lives had been her passion. She loved to see the small faces every day, to help them decipher words and learn their numbers, to celebrate with them when they finally understood a problem, and to comfort them when they just could not make sense of it. But after forty years, the shine had worn off. Every year, her budgets were cut, the children got more obnoxious, and the parents became more demanding. She was sick of listening to parents describe their children as prodigies when, at best, they were average. Sick and tired of them blaming her for their own shortcomings.

And now this new head teacher had arrived with his trendy ideas and "safety first" approach. His youth and inexperience protruded from every orifice, with his brightly coloured ties and trendy trainers instead of the smart shoes she was used to male colleagues wearing. She was beginning to acknowledge that she might be getting too old for this or that maybe teachers never actually became too old and that instead they are simply driven out by their younger counterparts, newly trained colleagues who don't adhere to dress codes and give out medals for participation. Practically children themselves, with their rolls of gold stars and their pedantic need to make sure everything is safe.

Every day of her teaching career, she had had her cups of coffee at the same time, regarding them as a personal prize for getting through that section of the day, and now that was being taken away. Rules about hot drinks and children; risk assessments about cups of coffee left on desks, ready to scald an unsuspecting infant. In reality, she was so busy that she hadn't had a hot cup of coffee at work in years.

The Incident

She briefly wondered about retirement, but she knew she couldn't afford it, not after her husband had upped and left to re-find his missed youth. Leaving her with two teenage children and a mountain of debts, debts they had built together in the search for the perfect life. But more importantly, if she did retire, what would she do? Her children had moved away; her eldest lived a high-powered life of luxury in the city, and her youngest travelled the world. If she stopped teaching, what would she get up for? The thought depressed her, but at least if she did retire, she could continue to have a cup of coffee when she wanted. It might even be hot.

She checked her watch and drained the last dregs of gritty instant coffee. "Good lord, what is she wearing today?" she heard her teaching assistant mutter. She immediately knew who the teaching assistant was referring to. Today the mother, the one everybody talked in hushed whispers about, was wearing some sort of brightly patterned floral dress and a denim jacket covered in patches. She was also carrying a large straw handbag, the kind you find lining the beach on holiday. "She looks like an explosion in a charity shop," the teaching assistant added, a cruel smile playing on her lips. The teacher gave her a stern glare and said, "that's quite enough".

The teacher felt oddly protective of this mother; she was exuberant, yes, with her wild clothes and her loud laugh, but she was kind. She always had a friendly smile and "good morning" for the other parents, a tray of baking for the cupcake sale, and her son was obviously well cared for. So why should people judge? Plus, she didn't like the teaching assistant. She was a PTA mum who had managed to wrangle a job in the school so she could keep an eye on her own children and generally make life more unpleasant for the teachers. Briefly, the teacher wondered if the colourful mother was looking for a job. She would swap the two of them in a heart-beat.

The Old Man

The old man sat in his living room, waiting patiently. He had already gone through the laborious process of getting himself dressed for the day, forcing stiff limbs to bend against their will into armholes, and the precarious task of standing on one weak leg to put on his trousers and underpants. He had lightly dusted the silver-framed photograph of his late wife, like he did every morning. As an ex-military man, he was a creature of habit. Taking the same breakfast every morning and wearing the same combination of clothes. Trousers, shirt, and tie all neatly pressed in a spectrum of blues, with a pullover in the winter and a straw fedora in the summer. At approximately half past eight every morning, after his cup of tea, he would take himself down to the bottom of the garden for his first cigarette of the day.

His late wife hadn't liked him smoking, but a lifetime of the habit had made it impossible for him to give up, so every day, morning, lunch time, dinner time, and just before bed, he had snuck off to the bottom of the garden for what he thought was a sly smoke. He had hidden behind the shed, and his wife had pretended not to notice what he was doing or where he was disappearing off to.

It occurred to him that now that she had passed, he could smoke whenever and wherever he wanted. He didn't have to walk down to the bottom of the garden, negotiating tufts of weeds and knocking pieces of litter out of his way with his stick so they wouldn't get under his feet and risk the thing that all geriatrics fear the most, a fall.

He could even smoke in the house if the mood took him. But the thought of ruining his wife's carefully chosen cushions and curtains with the stench of tobacco put him off. Moreover, years of routine meant he never craved cigarettes at any other times of the day apart from the stolen moments he had carefully allotted to himself over the course of his marriage. He took a long, slow drag and listened carefully. Any moment now, he would hear the faint sound of the school bell on the wind, and five minutes later, he would see her.

Their acquaintance had started small. She had given him a cheery wave one day and wished him a wonderful day. Not "good morning," no, that would be too banal, too generic. She had instead said, "I hope you have a wonderful day," and for the first time since his wife's death, he had indeed tried to have a wonderful day, as if the woman's sentiment had finally given him the strength to try. He started to read his favourite book again, and he took his old bones outside to begin tidying the garden.

His wife had been very proud of the garden, and since her death he had let it become overgrown and untidy. After the first hello, he felt a renewed vigour. He began to pull up the plethora of weeds, exposing the flowers his wife had planted years before and giving them room to grow properly. The garden became the next thing he and the young woman spoke about. She had commented on how beautiful his poppies were and had asked if he would mind if she had some of the seeds for her own garden when they were ready. He hadn't minded her directness, and a sort of small, tentative friendship was formed.

They had become quite familiar. Every day she stopped and said hello, and they spoke for a while, sometimes about their favourite books, or the flowers, or the weather. Sometimes the old man had even commented on what she was wearing, noting how rare it was to see a young woman in a dress nowadays and what lovely bright colours she had chosen. Secretly, he loved the way she dressed best. It reminded him of his wife in her youth, with her gathered skirts billowing around her on the dance floor.

He wondered if today would be the day he broke from his routine and asked her in for a cup of tea. So far, he had chickened out, but in truth, he was lonely. He wondered if the young woman would be offended if he asked her in for a beverage. Or, if heaven forbid, she would be scared. After all, he was basically a stranger. His wife would have invited the younger woman over in a heartbeat. His Maureen had had a knack for making friends. She was always inviting people over for cups of tea. She had no regard for the plans that she and the old man might have made the night before. She was quite happy to disregard their schedule for a cup of tea and a natter with a friend, or a potential friend, and he loved her for it.

The Watcher, the Waiter, the Hunter

She would be done soon; she always spoke to the old man, laughing and throwing her hair over her shoulder. Then she would shout him a cheery farewell, wishing him a wonderful day or an excellent week, and finally she would take the same path through the trees that she took every morning on the way back home, and he would see her.

He had seen her every day. He had watched; he had noted how she always held the little boys left hand and how she would reassure him when the dog walker came past with his stupid bloody mutt. He saw how she would lightly jump across the puddle that always pooled in the centre of the path when it rained and how occasionally she would put in two tiny earphones to listen to music as she walked home, an extra spring in her step as she kept time with the music. He wondered what symphonies of sounds were emitted from the headphones to unconsciously make her feet dance.

He had noticed other things as well. That she walked every day, never taking the lifts home that other parents offered her, and that she never strayed from her usual route. He knew where she lived, how long it took her to get there, and what time her husband came home from work.

She had never noticed him; nobody noticed him. They were all too busy going about the mundane clockwork of their own lives. The neighbours hadn't even realised that his mother had died. He hadn't bothered to put a proper announcement in the local paper.

Mother didn't deserve it; she was a witch anyway. Always asking him why he wasn't better or why he wasn't just more. Why did he work such a pathetic job? Why didn't he go out with friends? Did he have any friends? Did he have a girlfriend? Why didn't he have a girlfriend? Why did nobody love him? Why wouldn't he give her grandchildren? A constant stream of whys.

She was a vile woman, filled with spite and malice. Accusing him of being useless and telling him he would never get what he wanted because he didn't have the balls. Well, he had the balls now mother. He had been watching, been waiting. He knew her habits, her routine, and he knew what he wanted.

He was nearly ready to make his move, and he was bursting with anticipation.

The Wife, the Mother, the Woman, the Victim

She had been taught at a young age by her mother that walking cleansed the soul. It was almost as good as yoga in that respect. She enjoyed the walk to school with her small son hanging on her arm, asking her for stories and songs. She also enjoyed the solitude of her walk home alone. She was a woman who was as comfortable in her own company as she was in the company of others. But these moments on the way home from school were hers and hers alone. No one could take them away from her; that's why she never took the lifts home that the other parents offered. She didn't want to be sat in the other parent's stuffy people carriers, surrounded by biscuit crumbs and spare socks, talking about school or housework. She wanted to be alone on her path, with her own thoughts and concerns.

Walking gave her the opportunity to think things through. Like what could she do to cheer up the old man? Every morning, he seemed so pleased to see her that she knew he must be lonely. She thought about inviting him to her house for a cup of tea, but what if the walk was too far for him? She wondered if he had any children to look after him. He had never mentioned having a child, but he talked about his wife often, describing in great detail her love of gardening and sunshine. He always referred to her as his darling late wife, with a sad smile spread across his face.

She wondered if her own husband ever talked about her in that way. She doubted it. Their marriage was the result of a courtship that was convenient, formed over one too many drinks that neither of them had the guts to end, and a condom that hadn't quite lived up to its advertisements and promises of safe sex.

Still, she wouldn't change her life. It was easy, if not a little monotonous, and she loved her son with all of her heart. But still, she couldn't stop the thought that not everything was as it should be and that she was missing something. Something was casting a shadow on her perfect life, and she couldn't put her finger on it.

The Watcher, the Waiter, the Hunter

She was here. The woman was here! He could see the outline of her figure as she cut through the trees and started down the path. His fingers began to itch, and he wondered if today was the day to put his plan into action. No, he steadied himself; a few more things needed to be put in order first. There could be no trail.

He wondered if he should treat himself to an interaction. He could start down the same path as her, walk briskly, and say a cheerful "good morning" as he had before. But again, he steadied himself, not today. He knew he would lose control. The first time she had spoken to him, after he had watched her for months, he had felt so elated that he had to scurry home without buying any milk so he could furiously masturbate in the floral spare room of his mother's house.

His mother had been furious about the lack of milk. She had called him useless, pathetic, and a waste of space. But her words couldn't touch him. He was walking on air. He was sure he had met the woman he was meant to spend the rest of his life with, or even just one heavenly moment. This must be what all of the musicians were singing about, what poets wrote about. What love at first sight means, knowing in your heart when someone is the one. Knowing that there is someone in the world that you love so much that you would do anything for them. Anything to have them.

The Wife, the Mother, the Woman, the Victim

The woman slowly removed her earphones, listening to the sounds of the outside world as the music faded away. The sounds of birds and wind replaced the melody. She had the unsettling feeling that she was being watched. It was ridiculous of course. This was hardly a city street where she could be followed. This was a short path, maybe twenty-five metres in length. Yes, it was covered on both sides, but there were houses on one side of the trees. She had walked this path a hundred times before. She was being stupid. Of course, it was safe. After all, nothing had happened yet, so why would anything happen at all?

That said, she still felt uncomfortable walking alone, so she pulled out her mobile phone and called her mother.

The Watcher, the Waiter, the Hunter

The man surveyed the woman and cursed quietly to himself. Bloody mobile phones. Everyone had one nowadays. Forever posting every little tedious detail of their lives on Facebook and Instagram, tweeting the intimate moments of their lives; what they had for breakfast, what they thought of the news, what their bloody relationship status was. He had a mobile, but nobody rang him.

If he checked his phone now it would show only two calls from the entire time he had owned it. One from the factory he used to work in to say he had left a pair of shoes in his locker and was wondering if he wanted to collect them or if they should just throw them away. And one from the police telling him his mother was dead. Nobody else rang him to check on him. He had no friends and no family now that his mother was gone.

When he and the woman got together, he was sure they would spend so much time in each other's company that there would be no need for mechanical devices. She would probably get rid of her phone, preferring instead to save all of her conversations and thoughts for him. The secrets that they would share wouldn't be described with emojis and numbers; they would use proper words. Only he would witness the small details of her life.

The mobile did pose an issue though, should his plan not go as he wanted. If he didn't have time to woo his lady love and explain his actions, then she might phone someone, and that would be a big problem. It could put him in a bad light. People might misunderstand; they might make unkind assumptions.

He took a pencil and notebook from his pocket and made a note on his to-do list. So far, it only contained four items: mother, job, dog, and woman. He added mobile phone and noted that only one thing was crossed off the list. Good job he hadn't lost his head and tried to put his plan into action today; he wasn't prepared.

Then he strained his ears to try and hear the woman's conversation. She was talking to her mum again. The hunter had watched her for so long that he knew she talked to her mother at least once a day, always in the morning and never when her husband was home.

The watcher couldn't understand the fascination other people had with their mothers. His own mother had been a thorn in his side. He was not one of those boys who was tied to his mother's apron strings. Even as a child he had tried to distance himself from her, and now he was glad to be rid of her.

He was so lost in thoughts about his own mother that he hadn't noticed the woman turn through the trees into the town. He had missed her final moments. But it was no matter. Farewell, my lady, he thought to himself. Not long now.

The Wife, the Mother, the Woman, the Victim

The rest of the woman's day went as it normally did. She made a cup of coffee as soon as she got home, filling her favourite mug to the brim with liquid energy, and started on her numerous chores. She always made sure to sort her husband's affairs before her own. She washed and ironed his shirts and tried to ignore the strange, spicy scent that clung to the fibres as she pulled them from the dirty laundry hamper. After that, she would collect her son from school, walking the same paths she always took, and then start dinner, hoping and praying that her husband wouldn't have to work over his hours. Yet again.

Tonight, there was no such luck. "Big order on... They need me here... I'll grab something to eat on the way home. No need to wait up." Subconsciously, she felt relieved; she wouldn't have to justify how she'd spent her day. He'd be home so late he wouldn't notice that she hadn't hoovered the carpets because she'd been reading her favourite book or that the sink was still full of last night's dishes because she'd binge watched reality TV, absorbing the mindless drama of the shows he hated.

Plus, it meant she could help her son with his reading. The child hated reading with his father. He stumbled over easy words, and more often than not, the activity ended in floods of tears. She had more patience with him. She understood that words were hard, that the letters never made the same sound twice, and that too much pressure could cause a child to crumble.

She put their son to bed, reading the child his favourite story and tucking the covers around his small frame like a shield. Then she sat downstairs with a glass of red wine, waiting for her husband to come home. When the clock struck twelve, she gave up and went to bed. Her husband was no Cinderella, and she wasn't his fairy godmother. She heard him come in a few hours later, creeping along the hallway in his socks like a teenager who was out past curfew. She wondered where he had parked his pumpkin, giggled to herself, and rolled over, pretending to be asleep.

The Day of the Incident

Our actions have a butterfly effect on the people around us. You kicking dandelions on your evening walk could mean that the owners of the houses nearby spend months trying to pull up weeds. Your complaint in a restaurant could result in the waitress being fired and not being able to afford to feed her children. The chewing gum you drop could end up on the shoe of a boy who will embed it into the carpet at his girlfriend's house, losing the approval of her parents forever. The paths of our lives are intertwined with those around us more deeply than we can ever imagine.

The Watcher, the Waiter, the Hunter

The watcher examined the notebook in his hand as he ate his measly breakfast. Everything was taken care of. He was hiding, camped out in the rotting shed at the bottom of his mother's garden, pretending not to exist. eating cold baked beans from the tin while sitting on his sleeping bag. Surrounded by flower pots and rat droppings. He slurped the rest of the juice from the can, being careful not to cut his mouth on the sharp edges, and dripped sticky tomato juice into his unkempt beard. The shed contained none of his personal belongings save a sleeping bag, a change of clothes, and a few old tins that he had taken when the council had asked him to remove his mother's belongings from the house.

His mother had few personal possessions. She was unsentimental, so there were no birthday cards or Valentine's Day cards from his father, no pieces of flimsy card expressing love, and he found no traces of his old school work, no record of his achievements as a child. Her room had only contained her few clothes and a well-worn bible, pages thumbed and frayed.

The council were coming later that day to finish emptying his mother's house and turn it over, ready for new tenants. He could already picture them, a scruffy family with a mish mash of illegitimate children. People who relied on the government for their housing and who had never done an honest day's work in their shallow, pathetic lives. Wastes of oxygen. Wastes of blood, muscle, and sinew.

The Incident

He had always worked, ever since he left school. Well, at least up until the summer, when the factory "regretfully had to let him go". The man who had fired him hadn't even gotten his name correct in the meeting, and he had a coffee stain on his tie. This was the course of events that had led him back to his mother's spare room and her wrath.

She had been unimpressed to find that her only son had no savings and no actual qualifications. He had worked the same factory job since leaving education and had had no promotions and no prospects. Gradually, over the years, all the spontaneity of his life had been sucked out of him. Friends no longer invited him for a cheeky pint down the pub, and dates with women had dried up.

He tried to remember the last time he'd had sex or been intimate with another human being. It was probably the busty woman who worked on the same factory line as him at the works Christmas party. He hadn't wanted to go, but he had been told it would be "fun" and that management were buying the first round of drinks. He had stuck to a shandy, but many people had ordered fancy cocktails, and so had the busty woman. She had slurped an unnatural blue liquid from a vessel more suited for holding aquatic life than alcohol, and the effects had hit her instantly. He couldn't recall her name, but she had become the sort of loud, awful drunk that people are when they have downed too much alcohol in a short space of time and have had nothing to eat. He had offered to drive her home safely. He hadn't drunk too much preferring to keep his senses sharp.

In the car, she had gone from loud and obnoxious to quiet and sleepy. Her round face paled slightly during the drive, and a sheen of sweat formed on her upper lip. He wondered if she might be sick, but she assured him that she felt fine, just tired. He had driven her to the address her friend had scribbled down on the back of a beer mat, and he had taken her keys from the bag to let her in. In her handbag, he saw the condoms that had spilled from her bag earlier while she had drunkenly wriggled around the dance floor. The woman seemed to forget the concept of opening doors and was having trouble standing as well, so he helped her, and whilst on the doorstep, she had given him a slurred thank you and a big wet kiss on his mouth.

The kiss was all he needed; years of being starved for affection had left him hungry and needy. He had taken her to bed that night and had sex with her. She hadn't said no. But it didn't stop nasty rumours spreading around the factory the next day. The women whispered behind their hands, using phrases like "took advantage" and "in no fit state to know what she was doing". Whilst the men laughed and said she was "always up for it" and "shouldn't have gotten herself into that state" they had all seen the condoms spill onto the dance floor, and they had gathered what type of woman she was. The busty woman had obviously been planning to have sex with someone. It just happened that he had been the lucky one.

The busty woman seemed embarrassed by the encounter. She avoided him on the line and never acknowledged the night they had spent together. Eventually, she quit. He was furious about her attitude. He had driven her home safely, taken her to bed, and loved her. He'd even washed up the dirty dishes in her sink and put her dress and underwear in the washing machine. Ungrateful bitch.

He struck the thoughts of the busty woman from his mind. This woman would be different. This wasn't a pathetic one-night stand. This was the making of the rest of his life. He'd worked so hard. Some things had been difficult, but it wasn't hard to cover his tracks. No one knew he lived with his mother. After the redundancy, she hadn't told a soul, fearing that her precious government benefits would be cut and that the neighbours would talk. "A man, nearly forty, crawling back to his mother's apron strings! It's an embarrassment." She had cried one night.

So, she had kept him secret, claiming he just came for visits to give her a helping hand. Never telling the council that her only son had moved into the spare room, that she supplemented her income with his redundancy money. She had whinged of course, he cost a fortune to feed, and she missed her quiet freedom. But he made himself useful by buying the milk for her tea every morning and administering her pills.

These pills were how he tied up another loose end and crossed an item off his to do list. Every morning, his elderly mother took two large painkillers to cope with the pain from her arthritis. Her old and twisted hands couldn't open the bottle. A child lock, blocking an adult woman from pain relief. Her son had stepped in and begun to administer the pills. She hadn't noticed when he had popped open the capsules and filled them to the brim with more powder. Nor had she noticed when he had poured the rest of her prescription into the milk for her tea.

He had worried that the three packets of heavy-duty painkillers he had found wouldn't be enough to make her drift away, especially since he needed the last packet for the rest of his project. But as it turned out, his mother had secrets of her own. Specifically, the large bottle of Irish whiskey she drank every day. The combination of whiskey and pills had taken his mother quietly to her death. It never occurred to him to check where the whiskey came from.

But the authorities did. Upon finding her body, they concluded that she had died due to taking too many tablets. "Old age makes people so forgetful, poor love" the paramedics had whispered, and by washing them down with large quantities of whiskey supplied to her by the teenager next door for a small fee. The paramedics had concluded that she must be lonely. After all, she lived alone and was probably trying to drink away her solitude. There was no trace of any other person in the house.

The teenager was not prosecuted. He had no knowledge of the lady's prescription; he just thought he was helping with her shopping. The information from the police showed he was a good boy who got caught at the wrong end of trouble while trying to help out a neighbour. What they didn't know was that he'd used the old lady's payments to start up his own drug dealing business, serving the small population of the town who just wanted to forget their troubles.

The son wasn't prosecuted either. As far as the police knew it was an unfortunate accident of old age. The investigators didn't notice that the twisted and gnarled hands of the old woman would be useless in opening the pill bottles, nor did they notice that the old woman was drinking milk freshly brought from the shop but that she was still in her flowered nightgown. Instead, they filled in the blanks of the case with their own carefully crafted truths and closed the investigation. They had given the watcher their condolences and left him able to get on with his plan.

The Wife, the Mother, the Woman, the Victim

The woman walked her son to school as she did every morning, hand in hand, smiling at the man in the suit and not even noticing the absence of the dog walker.

Her mind was elsewhere; between the singing of songs and the telling of stories. She tried not to think about the continuous buzzing noise her husband's phone had made all night. How he had shielded the screen as she walked past to get a drink. How he had turned off the vibrations after she had commented that he was "Mr Popular" that evening.

She had considered checking the phone but, she didn't have the pass code, and she trusted her husband, or at least she tried to. He was a good father and an excellent partner. He never forgot her birthday, and every year on their anniversary, 12 long stemmed roses were delivered. She tried to ignore the fact that she wasn't a fan of roses; they reminded her of funerals and that she would much prefer her favourite flowers, sunflowers or daisies, but still she appreciated the thought. He was a good man. He was to set in his ways to lie to her, too uptight to do something that might damage their marriage and too conscious of the opinions of others to do something to damage his spotless reputation. But still, a nervous voice at the back of her mind told her that she was missing something.

Suddenly she was taken by the thought that she should run away and start somewhere new with her son, maybe near the ocean. Just the two of them. She had always loved the tranquillity of the sea. Give up her normal life and become a pair of travelling gypsies, going only where the wind takes them. Make every day an adventure. She was sure there were friends who would take them in, old acquaintances who would open their doors and their hearts.

The gap in the trees brought her back to her senses. They were nearly at the school. Five more minutes, and they would be there. She would drop off her son and have the whole day to debate her existence and the choices she had made.

The Owners of the Terrace

The man in the terrace slept soundly in his bed for the first time in months. His wife's snoring wasn't there to wake him, as she had an early shift at the hospital, and he had finally heard the news that his job was safe. The relief he felt was overwhelming.

Months of redundancies had left him tossing and turning at night. Wondering how he would pay the mortgage every month, how he would afford his and his wife's traditional Friday night take away without a job. No noise from the outside world or the world inside his head disturbed his sleep.

And the window was closed.

The ~~Dog~~ Walker

Unlike previous days of his life, the dog walker was not awoken by the warm, wet licks of his dog. His Bella, his gentle giant, had been poisoned the day before. The vet couldn't be sure, but she thought it was some sort of heavy dose of painkillers, lethal to humans in large quantities and equally, if not more lethal to dogs, but irresistible when stuffed into a large meaty sausage.

The dog walker had no idea who had hurt his beloved animal. He assumed it was one of the people who considered the breed to be dangerous and thought they should be banned. Maybe it was even the man who had shouted from the terrace one morning. He wished whoever had done it could see the empty gap it had left in his life. He no longer needed to walk down the woodland path each morning. He wouldn't see people cross to avoid the dog or hear the single, solitary hello of the young woman. An act of unspeakable cruelty had altered his life forever.

He turned over in bed and caught sight of his face in the mirror. He took another one of the sleeping tablets the doctor had prescribed him a long time ago, when every day had been a struggle and he had been plagued with thoughts of suicide and depression. The days before he had his dog.

She had arrived in his life collarless and barking at his back gate. He had been considering taking a fist full of pills to numb the pain inside, to finally end things. But the dog kept interrupting, so in the end he had given up and taken her to the vets to find her owner. When the vet had checked, she found no information on the dog's chip, and no one had placed a missing advert anywhere. He had visited her every day at the kennels, bringing her treats, toys, and a blanket from his own bed to keep her warm at night.

It was the first time he felt useful. The dog gave him a reason to get up in the morning, to get dressed, and face the day. After a few weeks of waiting, no owners turned up, and he offered to adopt her. The city kennels had waived the adoption fee, knowing that the man and the dog had already made a deep-rooted connection and he had taken her home. When he thought that a dog might have saved his life he chuckled. But it was true; he no longer felt the need to spend all day in bed staring at the ceiling. He got a haircut, found a job, and spent his mornings walking his beloved dog.

Well, he used to. As the sleeping tablet took hold, the ex-dog owner rolled back over, hoping to waste the day away in deep slumber, wondering quietly to himself how his life had come full circle.

The Watcher, the Waiter, the Hunter

He had spent the night barely sleeping in the small shed, he had been uncomfortable, yes. Old tools had dug into the fleshy parts of his body, and rats had run around his feet in the night, upsetting his dreams. But he had also been thinking about the moment that led him to this path.

The first morning he saw her. It must have been the start of a new school year, and a woman he had never seen was walking down the woodland path, holding the hand of a nervous child. She was offering words of comfort to the child, reassuring him that he was going to have a brilliant day. The watcher had tried to recall if his own mother had ever offered him words of comfort or if she had ever interwoven encouragement with her venom and malice. She hadn't.

The watcher had paused on the path, pretending to be looking at the trees but really transfixed by the woman's clothes. He was an old-fashioned man; he liked women to dress like women. He hated seeing young girls in the shops shrouded by layers of sweatshirts and jumpers. Ill-fitting clothes.

He hated women in jeans; he liked to see a woman's legs. You could see this woman's legs, bare despite the cold, and every now and again, a gust of wind would lift the hem of her dress a little higher. Exposing more pale, creamy flesh. If he looked carefully, he could see goose pimples decorating them whenever a breeze took hold. He wondered how far up her legs the goose pimples went and felt his face burn in the cold breeze.

He had shuddered on the path; exhilaration ran through him, and whilst listening to the high tinkle of her laugh, he knew. This was the woman for him. After his stroll down memory lane, the watcher got up and began the preparations for his day.

The Wife, the Mother, the Woman, the Victim

As they crossed the final main road towards the school, the woman noticed that her son was more animated than usual. He hadn't stalled on the woodland path. She put this down to a good mood, not thinking that it might have something to do with the missing dog that normally terrified him.

She gave him his usual kisses and cuddles as he lined up to go into school, using her actions to make sure her son knew how loved he was. She tried to make polite conversation with the other ordinary mothers, despite the fact that they normally snubbed her, and she waved cheerily to his teacher as she came to take the class in. Then, after the final school bell had rung, she turned on the spot, a pirouette fit for a ballerina and started her walk home. A colourful mess of fabric fluttering out behind her in the wind.

The Old Man

He'd heard the school bell ring. So, he removed his slippers and put on his gardening shoes. A glance at the calendar told him his only son would ring today. His son always rang on Wednesdays. The old man hated these conversations; his son would make the forced exchange of someone who was secretly ashamed of where he had come from, the edge of poverty in which he had grown up. His son was conveniently forgetting the love that had filled their small home and the sacrifices that had been made so he could have the things he needed. His son hated that his father was old. He hated the way his father's back was crooked where it was once ramrod straight. He believed him to be incapable of living alone, and inevitably, at some point in the conversation, he would bring up the idea of some care home or retirement community.

"A prison more like!" The old man would snap down the phone. He was perfectly happy where he was, thank you, surrounded by the memories of his beloved wife, and of their life together. Of their youth. If he moved, he wouldn't be able to take half of his things, half of her things. The flowered Pyrex dishes they had been given as a wedding gift from his favourite aunt would be redundant with staff to make his meals, and the writing desk that Maureen had written thank you notes at wouldn't fit into whatever hamster cage his son found for him.

He had seen these kinds of places before; all of his friends had ended up in them. Surrounded only by old photos, with sternly, smiling nurses giving them orders, telling them when they could have a cup of tea or an extra biscuit. Constantly checking their blood pressure, monitoring their moods on clipboards, and writing down every bowel movement, every fall, and every accident. He had seen what places like that had done to his friends, how they had sucked the life out of them and diminished their souls until they were less than people, more like overgrown pets, and he was sure they died faster because of them.

He took himself outside, wondering if he should just ignore the phone call later and save himself the bother. His wife had adored their only child. After three miscarriages she considered him to be a wonderous gift from God, and as a result, she had spoiled him and indulged in his every whim.

She had scrimped to send him to the local grammar school and insisted that they pay for as much of his university as they could. "He's the first in the family to get a degree love, we should be proud of him, and we don't want him starting out his life with a mountain of debt". It had never occurred to the son to pay his parents back after he took a job managing a bank. Instead, he relied on his secretary to write cards and send flowers on his mother's birthday and took long holidays in the sun with women he didn't bother to introduce to his parents. He never brought these women to the house, even though his mother had asked him over and over again. She wanted to meet these women to see if they might be suitable mothers for her hypothetical grandchildren. But they never met them, and grandchildren were never discussed, never created. Their son kept them both at arm's length. He was ashamed of his roots, ashamed of the small bungalow his father continued to keep and the old, worn-out furniture that occupied it.

He saw the woman rounding the corner and waved to her. She commented once again on how lovely his flowers were and how he must be taking excellent care of them in the weather. The old man toyed once again with the idea of inviting her in for a cup of tea, but yet again lost his nerve. Instead, he only said goodbye and went back to his day. Inside the house the phone rang with his weekly phone call. He answered it right away. After all, aside from the woman, his son was his only contact with the outside world. It wouldn't do to have him worry.

The Watcher, the Waiter, the Hunter

She was coming. He had seen her say goodbye to the old man, and soon she would cut through onto the woodland path. As always, she was wearing a dress, an impractical light cotton fabric covered in a pattern of large tropical flowers. He adjusted his position slightly; all he needed to do was make sure she couldn't reach her phone. Then he would be able to execute his plan without interruption.

Excitement tingled through his body; his heart felt like thunder in his chest, roaring, trying to break out of the restraints of his skin. He had thought everything out so carefully and today was the day. He'd been rock hard since the morning and had already skilfully rolled on a condom, ignoring the pleading of his body to have one moment of pleasure before he left to find the woman. He didn't want to ruin the moment by messing about with a condom when they were finally together or by failing to perform due to an ill-timed act of self-gratification this morning. All of his waiting had led him up to this moment, and he wanted it to be perfect. It had to be.

The Wife, the Mother, the Woman, the Victim

The sun was glinting through the trees as she cut down on to the path. Some beads of dew were sitting on top of the blades of grass, and a cold breeze shook the branches of the trees. There was no one else there, and it was peaceful and serene.

Lost in nature, the woman hardly noticed the soft footsteps behind her. She started suddenly when she felt her handbag lifted from her hand, but the shock of the moment stopped her from crying out. She was greeted with a bearded face who smiled sweetly as he threw the handbag just out of reach towards the roots of the trees and grabbed her arm with a firm hand.

Before she knew it, she was pulled to the floor, and unfamiliar hands were exploring her body. She let out one solitary scream before the man placed a gloved hand over her mouth, silencing her.

The Owner of the Terrace

The owner of the terrace continued to sleep deeply, lost in pleasant dreams. He hadn't heard the woman's scream. His window was firmly closed.

The Watcher, the Waiter, the Hunter

This was glorious. It had gone smoother than he had imaged; she had fallen to the floor with the grace of a ballerina when pushed and had only let out one small scream before he had to silence her. In his dark and twisted mind, he presumed the scream was of shock or ecstasy. He'd heard her fucking her husband on the nights he had sat watching and waiting outside of her home. He'd heard her chorus of moans and groans. He knew she could be very vocal when she was enjoying herself.

He removed as much clothing as he needed to, quickly, not able to control himself or relish the moment. After he had entered her, he'd started to gain rhythm rapidly. He willed himself not to come too fast. He wanted to savour the moment, and to have the opportunity to gaze into her eyes, which he was sure would be filled with love and gratitude.

He was touching her, grasping for exposed skin. He'd already ripped the strap of her summer dress, exposing lace and flesh. He couldn't believe it was happening. After they had finished, he was sure they would lie together, cocooned in the woodland path, surrounded by a blanket of leaves left by mother nature, and he would lovingly explain to her how he had watched her, and how he had waited. She would smile, and thank him for saving her, and cover his face and body with a million soft kisses.

She would tell him she would leave her husband, and they would start afresh together. With no mother or husband to spoil things. The child might be an inconvenience, but for their love, he was sure she could leave him behind. The husband could have him or the mother with whom she was always talking on that blasted phone. After all, they could have their own children; a whole brood of infants started from this first incredible moment of love if she desperately wanted to. Half him and half her, a perfect blend of their DNA. He'd worn a condom this time, but only because he didn't want her body ruined by pregnancy immediately. He wanted to have time to appreciate the curves he had only seen from a distance and bask in the skin, which he always imagined would be warm and smooth.

He looked down at her face and saw tears filling her eyes and spilling down onto her cheeks. He was taken aback; they weren't the tears of gratitude he was expecting. Her entire face was contorted in fear, loathing, and disgust. This wasn't right. He had watched endless hours of pornography. He had read the books that women always raved about as being sexy and romantic. Women liked strong men who took what they wanted. He had read it, and he had seen it. Why did she look scared, this wasn't right? Wasn't he doing it properly?

He was angry now. Hot venom flooding his veins. He had planned this for her, for their life together. He had taken great risks. Taken gambles that she would never understand or fathom. He started moving quicker, wanting this to be over, wondering how things had gone so wrong so fast. This was supposed to be love at first sight, the start of his life, the start of their life. Instead, the woman who was supposed to embrace him with loving, open arms was pushing hard against his chest. She was fighting back.

The ungrateful bitch. This wasn't right, not after he had watched and waited for so long. Not after he had done away with his wretched mother so they could start fresh and killed off the bloody dog so they wouldn't be interrupted. He deserved this prize.

She was straining more now; muffled sobs were coming through his fingers. Suddenly, he was scared. This wasn't romance. The night with the busty woman from the factory had been more romantic than this. He had lit scented candles after he'd carried her to bed. He had unwrapped the layers of her clothing like a present, taken his time, and basked in every inch of her body.

But surprisingly, this wasn't so awful. He was still touching her, still getting what he wanted. To his surprise, the woman struggling made him more excited. He had thought she was already his, but clearly, he would have to fight for what he wanted. He continued with his pounding and began to go faster and faster.

The Wife, the Mother, the Woman, the Victim

The woman had often considered what she would do in a real emergency situation. How would she react when forced to confront the horrible? Would she freeze? Would her palms sweat and her knees shake? Or would she rise to the occasion? Whilst watching movies, she tried to hold her breath when the heroine dived under water to try and save herself, wondering if she herself could cope without the luxury of oxygen. She had watched zombie films, wondering if she could run as fast and as long as the characters would. She assumed the adrenaline would help. Her husband had always laughed at her musings, saying she was weak and delicate and would be the first to die. On the other hand, he would be a lone survivor, a lord of empty cities and king of a barren world.

For the first few moments of the rape, she had lain in shock, in astonishment at the act that was happening to her. After her initial scream, he had covered her mouth and silenced her disbelief. His hands were probing as they pulled at the clothing she had chosen that morning, and fear kept her pinned to the ground. She was so frozen she didn't even realise she was crying, until she felt the wet spill of tears onto her cheeks and the sting of melted mascara in her eyes.

This man was taking advantage of her. This man, whom she had never seen and who she didn't know. He was penetrating the parts of her she had promised to her husband. His beard was attacking the soft skin of her face, skin she cared for every night with scented creams and oils. The harsh hairs were scratching her, trying to work their way under the surface like wire wool. He was rubbing her raw, her insides and her outsides.

Suddenly, something inside her snapped. This bastard was trying to worm his way into every inch of her. His sweat was pouring from him, dripping, and her pores were soaking it in. She didn't want any more of his essence inside her. It was her body, and he was possessing it, roughly and without mercy.

She tried screaming again. But only muffled grunts managed to escape the gloved hand over her mouth. This encouraged him. She wondered if he had a weapon, a knife or a gun, if he might kill her. Now, during, or after. She tried to remember if there had been any guidance about this at school.

Don't walk alone at night, don't dress like a whore, don't get too drunk. Be ladylike, don't put yourself in a situation where you might get raped. Well, it was daytime, still the first fold of morning. She was wearing a tea-length dress, the sort of thing her grandma might have worn for a dance during the war, and she wasn't drunk. She hadn't touched a drop of alcohol in years.

As for location, she was on the edge of a town, her own home town. She could see the tops of houses peeking through the trees, houses she had seen a thousand times. Closed floral curtains blocked her from the worlds of the residents within.

The rules for not getting raped had been drilled into her, and she had abided by them. But nothing had been said about if you were actually being raped. If some large, looming figure had actually managed to get you on the floor and remove the French lace knickers you had taken from your dresser drawer that morning. If they ripped your dress and held you down. If they made it feel as though you had no choice and it seemed as though help was nowhere to be found.

Should she lie there? Hope against hope that if she was quiet and good that it would be over soon and he might leave her alive, walk off down the path like he had done nothing to ruin her day, to ruin her life. Should she fight back and risk that he had a knife? Something else that he could plunge into her body and drain the life out of her with. She might die. He might kill her. Leave her son motherless, leave her husband a widow, and leave her parents childless. Finish and slit her throat so she couldn't tell anyone. She'd heard that some men liked that sort of thing, to kill a woman as they came. It gave them pleasure.

Or he might leave her there on the floor, feeling naked, dirty amongst the rocks and mud. He might run, the soft footsteps that had surprised her turning into a frenzied gallop. He might do this again; he might hurt someone else. Some other poor, helpless woman who was just going about her day, who hadn't in a million years expected this.

Fuck it. The woman started to push back on his chest, trying to shove him off her. She continued to try and scream. She tried biting down on the hand that covered her mouth, but the glove stopped it hurting him. There was a barrier between her freshly brushed teeth and the fleshy hand within. That or he was so carried away with the moment that he didn't notice her trying to maim him. Trying to sink her fangs into his skin, like a savage dog.

She tried kicking her legs, noticing that the more she fought back, the angrier he looked and the faster he went. He actually looked like he might kill her in that moment. She briefly considered stopping fighting so she wouldn't be hurt further. But then, in a moment of blissful clarity, she realised she felt like she was dying anyway, and she continued her battle.

The Watcher, the Waiter, the Hunter

She was fighting more now, twisting and turning. He couldn't get to her face to try to calm her with kisses. She was kicking her legs and trying to push him back away from her. She wasn't playing fair; she was ruining his moment. She was scrambling now, fighting with the frenzy of a trapped animal. In this moment he realised she wasn't beautiful. Her mouth, which normally smiled was trying to escape his hand. She was snarling and slobbering like a monster. The alabaster skin he had admired from a distance was flushed and angry, her pale face mottled with rage. A pattern of scratches already appearing on her cheeks, like a rash.

She didn't look beautiful; she looked vile, like a witch or a whore, the types of women his mother had warned him against. Loose women, those without morals. This wasn't what he wanted. He wanted her peaceful and serene, like he'd seen her countless times walking down the woodland path.

He looked around, searching for a way to fix the problem and make this closer to what he had imagined. He understood now that the romance he had been playing in his head wasn't going to happen. She wasn't worthy, in fact, she was less worthy than the busty woman at work. She was a whore. She didn't deserve his love, but she would receive his body. He wasn't finished.

He still wanted to have her, to finish what he had started. After all, he was the one who'd done all the planning and preparation. He deserved this. He glanced at the area surrounding them. He still had her pinned to the floor, but she was fighting back with more and more vigour. There was nothing he could see to help him. Years of responsible walkers had left no broken bottles, no shards of glass that he could use to threaten or plead, there was no rope from fly tipping or broken rocks. He should have brought a knife, but he didn't think he'd need it. He was so sure that this would be the first day of their lives together, that after he had his way with her, she would fall grateful and weeping into his arms and he would save her from her own tepid existence.

As she continued to struggle under the mass of his body, he made his decision and removed his hand from her mouth. The quiet shock on her face showed hope that he was stopping or had finished. That her nightmare was over and she would be free at last. The wish was etched across her face and stopped her from screaming. Like a mouse being tormented by a cat, she was hoping he'd had his fun and would now leave her to pick up the pieces of her life.

But instead, he placed one hand on either side of her head as gently as a lover and slammed it down onto the path below. She was knocked out cold almost immediately, and he was free to continue with his plan.

He began again with renewed energy. This was almost better than her being awake. He could pretend that her eyes were closed with passion rather than pain, and after he was done, he could imagine she was in a blissful sleep, exhausted by their passionate encounter. He finished quickly and bit down on the soft flesh of her neck to stop himself from groaning too loudly. Then he pulled himself out of her and began to rethink the rest of his plan.

Originally, he had wanted to put her into the car and drive the 100 miles to the flat he had secured. Yes, she might protest; she might miss her family or the familiarities of her surroundings, but he was sure that they could soldier through. He was sure his devotion could convince her.

He understood now that it would be impossible. She didn't love him; she had teased him with her body and her beauty, then fought him. As much as he had enjoyed the thrill of possessing her, he also understood that to take her against her will would be dangerous. He slid off the now full condom and tied a knot in it, not noticing that a few small droplets of fluid that had fallen onto the woman's colourful dress, melting into the pattern of flowers and tropical leaves and becoming part of the fabric itself. He put the condom in his pocket. He kept the gloves on, glad that he'd had the foresight to wear them just in case. He'd dispose of everything later. But for now, he was assured that he had taken just enough precautions to keep himself out of trouble.

There may be small particles of DNA at the scene, but not enough to relate to him. After all, he'd never been in trouble before and the police had no record of him. In fact, as far as any authorities knew, he wasn't even in the area. He'd been fired from the factory; he had no ties to his mother's address and he'd been renting his new flat in another town for a month. He had a residence far from here. He had roots.

Clearly, their previous brief interactions had meant very little to her; they had made no impact on her life or her memory. Her face as she had first turned to see him, had been blank. It had hurt him to see no recognition in her eyes after all the time he had spent watching her. After all the attention he had paid her.

He wondered how long they'd been there on the path and thanked his lucky stars that, as of yet, no one had stumbled across them. He decided it wouldn't be too dangerous to take a few moments longer to savour everything, especially since he had waited so long for it.

He laid her legs out straighter, noticing the prickle of stubble; clearly, they were not as smooth as he had imagined. He pulled the skirt of her dress down to stop her from looking so exposed. He pocketed her underwear as a memento. He'd never seen underwear like it. It was lace and silk, a huge contrast to the enormous cotton pants he had laundered for his mother and the tacky diamante thong he had removed from the body of the busty lady.

He wasn't sure taking them was the best thing for his safety, but he couldn't bear to leave them behind, and a small voice in the back of his head said that the woman probably wouldn't want them any more anyway.

Lastly, he straightened the bodice of her dress, taking care to cover the breast he had pulled free earlier, and tucked her hair behind her ear, revealing where he had bitten her. A bruise was already threading its way onto the surface of her pale skin. It was at this point, the woman stirred, moving her head slightly to the side. The hunter noticed a pool of blood underneath her skull, already soaking into the gravel and matting into her hair.

Finally, the hunter realised the danger he was in. Slowly and calmly, he walked away. Feeling elated and a little scared.

The Wife, the Mother, the Woman, the Victim

The woman tried to raise her head from the ground. It hurt, it felt wet, warm, and heavy. She tried to remember where she was, the ground beneath her was hard, and she could feel a painful throbbing in her crotch. Surely she wasn't in bed; this wasn't the mattress she and her husband had chosen. Bickering in the store about firmness, her embarrassing him by asking the shop assistant how much bouncing the springs could take with a mischievous glint in her eye. This was earth, dirt, and nature.

Suddenly, it all came back to her. The man, the attack, what had happened. She went to sit up, but a wave of nausea hit her like a train. She needed help. She tried to scan the area. Was he still there? Had he gone? Was she safe?

Her phone, she needed her phone; human contact would save her. She half crawled and half dragged herself across the dirt, retching as she went to where he had thrown her handbag. Using the roots of the hundred-year-old tree to pull herself closer. Finally, she reached it and pulled her phone from the bag. In that instant, she knew exactly who she needed, the one person whose strength and stability would make her feel safe again. The wife phoned her husband.

The Husband

The husband was sitting in his car outside of his workplace. He was taking an unscheduled break when his phone rang, and the screen flashed up his wife's name. A goofy photo she had taken of herself on the phone before he had made it a fortress filled the screen. He ignored the call.

The Wife, the Mother, the Woman, the Victim

He wasn't answering. How could he not answer his phone? It was normally glued to his palm; he carried it around the house like a needy child. He answered phone calls during dinner, read texts while using the bathroom, and replied to emails in the dead of night. She'd heard him, the blunt noise of his finger tips hitting the glass screen, the snapping of his magnetic case opening and closing. It was impossible that he was apart from his phone now; they were never separated. She tried again.

Yet again a serene woman with a robotic voice told her to leave a message after the tone. So she tried again, and again. Till death do us part, in richness and in health. Where did sexual attacks fall into their vows? She tried again to phone him, lying on the floor listening to the phone ring whilst her vision swayed. It was too much to bear. Finally, the wife gave up, and the victim began to cry.

The Husband

"For fucks sake" a voice angrily rang through the plush interior of the parked car. His assistant had finally had enough of the interruptions and had stopped sucking his dick. The husband sighed, exasperated, and frustrated. He apologised about the phone calls, hoping to lose her in the moment once again so he could finish.

He checked his phone and debated turning it off. He had seven missed calls. His wife never normally rang him at work; it could be an emergency. She could have locked herself out again or left a tap running and flooded the bathroom. It wouldn't be important, but it might be; he should ring her back. His assistant turned to him, and the expression on her face cemented his decision. He swiftly turned the phone off.

Naturally, she was furious about the constant phone calls that had interrupted their precious time together. Their affair had started playfully enough, but now she was getting more and more demanding. She no longer wanted stolen moments at the office; she wanted flowers and hotel rooms. She was talking about taking a holiday together at some point, and she had pointedly mentioned that her parents were visiting soon and how much they were hoping to meet him. She wanted romance and a proper relationship. She wanted it all.

They had started out small. She had replaced his previous assistant, an old battle axe of a woman, who wore clumpy shoes and had short iron-grey hair that didn't move no matter what the weather did to it. He had hated his previous assistant with her filo fax and egg sandwiches eaten at her desk directly outside of his office, the smell drifting in and making him feel queasy.

He had been desperate to get rid of her, so he had fabricated some lies to the management, small things about files going missing and her ineptitude with the new computer system. He claimed she was too old and she was hindering his work, so the management suggested early retirement, and she gracefully took it, claiming she wanted to spend more time with her grandchildren. As it turned out, her daughter had other plans and had moved the grandchildren to Australia, leaving his old assistant widowed and alone. To relieve his guilt, he had brought her a massive bouquet of roses as a leaving present. After all, women love roses.

His new assistant had been a breath of fresh air. She wore high heels with short skirts and semi sheer blouses that barely concealed the lace bras she wore. She had been attentive and efficient from the first moment, always making sure his coffee was hot and ready on his desk. Remembering that he took it black, with one sugar after being told just once.

Things had escalated quickly; a well-placed hand on his arm had turned into one on his leg. A lingering look had become an outright seductive stare, and then one night she played her trump card.

They had exchanged phone numbers a week before so that he could text her the details of some work that needed doing, and she had accidentally sent him a naked picture, claiming it was for someone else. He'd tried to ignore it; in his heart, he wanted to be faithful to the wife he had ended up with. But after a day of his assistant flirting with him and coming home to a kitchen covered in flour and butter after his wife and son had been baking, he had lost his temper.

The house was filthy. Clearly, his wife had no regard for how hard he worked. How he yearned to come home to a tidy house and a nice, normal wife who didn't dress like a rodeo clown or draw looks in the supermarket. He had been hoping for a blazing row, for her to storm from the house and tell him to go fuck himself, the way she would have done when they first started dating, when their relationship was filled with passion and fire. Instead, she had nodded, and cried and told him she would do better. Years of his control had made her a shell of the woman she was before. Then she quietly cleaned the kitchen to spotless perfection. She had surrendered. He liked that; finally, she had surrendered. Now she was truly his.

The next day, when his assistant came up to him with her sex appeal and her smile, he caved and screwed her quickly on the desk, the same desk his wife had helped him choose when he was promoted. And now she was making noises about him leaving his wife and about when they would finally be together. He wasn't sure if that was what he wanted at the moment, to trade his wife, his son, and his home for a new adventure with a woman he barely knew but at the same time, he was forced to acknowledge that he had just turned off his phone and silenced his wife.

In the bubble of the car, he gave his assistant the words she wanted to hear: that he would leave his wife, that he would love to go on holiday with her, that he would meet her parents and that one day he would marry her. In gratitude for his empty words, his assistant began to finish the task she had started earlier. Another victory belonged to him.

The Wife, the Mother, the Woman, the Victim

Now the phone was going straight to voicemail. She tried to reason that maybe he was busy, but in her head, she knew that after that many missed calls, any normal husband would be panicking. It wasn't as though she normally rang him at work. In fact, typically they didn't talk during the day until he came home, demanded his dinner, and started picking fault with the state of the house. Lately, more often than not, these confrontational interactions had been longer apart than usual. He'd been working longer hours; there seemed to be countless birthdays and leaving dos which meant he'd have to go for drinks after work. Sometimes he wasn't even home for their son's bedtime. She was now in sole charge of bath time and stories, and she loved it.

She reasoned with herself and tried to sit up again. She felt something trickle down her neck and realised it was blood. The wound on the back of her head was worse from the motion of crawling across the gravel ridden floor. She picked her phone back up to ring nine, nine, nine. She knew she should have done it before, but in the shock of waking up on a gravel path, without underwear and a pounding head, all she had wanted was the comfort of her husband.

Now she was sure she needed proper help and started to dial the numbers as the phone swam around in front of her eyes. She'd typed two digits when the phone died; she should have charged it last night. Her husband had reminded her countless times, asking what she would do if she was in a car accident and needed to call someone. Well, here she was in an accident with no car in sight. Just then, she heard feet thundering down the path. She froze, hoping that it wasn't the hunter back again to torture her further.

The Man in the Suit

The man in the suit walked quickly down the path, occasionally breaking into a run. He was conscious that moving too rapidly would result in dark sweat stains on his grey suit, but he needed to be fast.

The blonde woman he had taken home from the bar last night had stolen two hundred pounds from his wallet. Two hundred pounds that had been given to him over the previous three weeks by his colleagues for his very pregnant coworker. He hadn't realised it was missing in the morning. He had only registered that his one-night stand had left slyly in the middle of the night and felt relieved; he wouldn't have to suffer through an awkward interaction where she tried to make more of their encounter than was actually there.

Upon reaching the office, he opened his wallet to stuff the cash into the card that had been repeatedly passed around the office for signing and noticed it was missing. "Bitch" he had muttered under his breath, knowing immediately that she was the culprit. No one else could have taken the money. He wished that for just once he had gone home alone, and now he was half running, half jogging, hoping to find a cash point so he could replace the money before the rest of the staff realised how much of an error he had made.

As he continued down the path, a violent, spasm of colour jarred his vision. A rainbow of colours juxtaposed against the natural shades of the woodland floor. Lying on the ground with blood saturated through her hair and the top of her dress ripped was the woman he saw with the child every morning. She looked at him, crying, so the mascara that was previously on her face now started to pool in her collar bones. She tried desperately to preserve her modesty by smoothing down the skirt of her dress, covering the trickle of blood that was cascading down her thigh. Then she spoke her first ever words to him as he held his breath. "Help me".

The Wife, the Mother, the Woman, the Victim

The man in the suit had phoned an ambulance and the police, she had been relieved to have seen a friendly face and happy to have some familiarity back in her life. The man was now sitting down next to her on the path, holding his suit jacket on the back of her head, like the emergency call centre woman had told him too. Her bleeding seemed to be stopping, but she had been violently sick on the man's shoes. The woman had worried that they might be expensive, but the man hadn't minded and kept reassuring her that the ambulance would be here soon.

He offered her a cigarette from a crumpled packet that he pulled from his trouser pocket, and she took it. She hadn't smoked in years; her husband claimed it was a filthy habit and had demanded she stop. But now, as she felt the first flurries of smoke hit her lungs, she felt a bit more grounded. She felt a bit more normal. Here was one thing she had control over: she might be putting poison into her body, but it was a poison she had chosen, not some strange man.

She heard shouting from around the corner and was suddenly surrounded by paramedics. She was carefully loaded onto a trolley and taken to the ambulance whilst the man in the suit stayed standing on the path, holding his bloody suit jacket in one hand. His other hand extended in a half-hearted farewell. The woman hadn't even had a chance to thank him and hadn't thought to ask his name. It was too late now.

The ambulance workers had taken her details quickly and were now driving her to the hospital. Blue flashing lights parted the traffic as the gravity of the morning's event finally weighed down on her, and she started to scream.

The Man in the Suit

The man in the suit returned to his office, pale and shaking. He had completely forgotten his crusade to replace the missing money. He walked through the doors to see his pregnant coworker announcing that her baby was going to be a little girl. The whoops and cheers stopped as soon as the pregnant woman saw him holding his now blood red suit jacket. She walked over to him, holding out her arms, and asked him what was wrong. He fell into them, and she held him against her ballooning belly. Mothering him in a way that he wouldn't have thought possible of a woman before she had born a child.

He cried. He openly wept in front of his colleagues, surrounded by pink balloons, bunting, and butter cream cake. He wept for himself, for the woman he had just helped, for the hundreds of women he had mistreated over the years, and for the baby girl in the stomach of the woman who now held him. He sobbed for an unborn girl who was about to enter into a world that was so cruel to women. And in that moment, he vowed to be different.

The Husband

The husband sat in the grey hospital hallway on an easy to wipe down plastic chair, drinking a foul polystyrene cup of coffee that a kind nurse had brought him. He hadn't seen his wife yet, and he had been anxiously waiting for an update ever since he heard the news.

His first instinct that something was wrong was when his manager had run across the car park. Normally, his fat, balding manager didn't leave the sanctuary of his office chair. Ruling the office from a leather imitation, ergonomically designed throne. But here he was running, his three chins wobbling and the girth of his stomach untucking his shirt as he took each step.

The husband had jumped out of the car before his manager reached him. He assumed it was about the affair, about the woman who was still sitting in his car, buttoning up her blouse and tidying her lipstick. Mentally, he started to come up with excuses; She had seduced him, he was having a breakdown, she was having a breakdown. Like a rat caught in a drainpipe he was going to struggle until his head was clear.

"It's the hospital, your wife," his manager wheezed, sweat dripping down from temples. Clearly, this wasn't about the affair. Hurriedly, whilst trying to catch his breath, his manager told him that the hospital had rung the office receptionist trying to reach him. There had been an incident with his wife. Members of staff had been running around for the past half an hour, trying urgently to find him, and in a moment of desperation, the manager had run to the car park to see if his car was still there or if he had already picked up the countless messages and left to attend to his wife at the hospital.

The husband stood in shock and turned his phone on. He had missed calls from his wife, from the hospital, and from his mother-in-law. Guilt flooded through his veins, and he froze on the spot "GO!" Shouted his manager, and so he turned and took the long strides towards his car. As the husband arrived at the motor, he saw his mistress sat primly in the front seat, oblivious to the news he had just received. He ordered her out of the vehicle, not stopping to give her details or an explanation of his actions, not even stopping to give her a kind word or look. As he left the car park, he saw the look of disbelief on his manager's face as he finally understood why they had struggled to find the husband for so long and why he had been in sitting in a parked car. His mistress stood next to him, her shirt buttoned up wrong, high heels in her hands, and a furious expression on her face.

A doctor walked down the hospital hallway, and the husband stood up. The doctor was holding a clipboard and a chewed pen. He began to calmly speak to the husband as if he were reciting his weekly shopping list; his wife had been attacked, her head had been split open and was being stitched back together now, she was under sedation because she had been screaming in the ambulance, and she had been raped.

The husband gasped at the word rape. Some beast of a man had explored areas of his wife that were his territory by marriage. Some foul being had his hands on his wife; he'd touched her, he'd violated her. The husband tried to concentrate on what the doctor was saying, but he found himself distracted by the chewed pen.

How could you be a medical professional and chew a pen? Surely only children chewed pens? Children and nervous people. He looked more intensely at the doctor, not really concentrating on what he was saying, and realised he was a lot younger than he had initially thought. Doubt flooded his mind; this must be a mistake. This idiotic youth must have mixed up the patient files. His wife was clumsy; she broke countless cups and glasses, she chipped the lips of beer bottles every time she opened them for him. She had probably fallen and hit her head, and this imbecile of a doctor had assumed she had been raped.

"That can't be correct" the husband interrupted the doctor. The doctor was taken aback. He assured the husband that it was correct. There were indications of rape, some vaginal bleeding, and trauma. The husband winced at the word vagina. His wife only called it her fairy or foof. She blushed at the anatomical name; she would hate to see that word on her charts. God, she would hate to know that these people, strangers she didn't know, had been looking down there. Investigating. God, he hated the thought of it himself.

His mother-in-law rounded the corner at full steam, she'd had further to travel. Like his wife, his mother-in-law was messy. She was wearing a moulting fur coat and a wide brimmed hat; she looked like an old film star who had fallen from grace and was desperate for attention. But once she reached the doctor, she was all business. She was asking the questions he should have asked himself. When would his wife wake up? Would she be in pain? Had they done the stitches? When would the police be here? The doctor answered his mother in laws questions promptly and professionally, then left politely. A tiny tuff of fur from her jacket had found its way onto the seat of his trousers and was hanging there like a small, limp comical tail.

The husband sat back down whilst his mother-in-law stood hand on hips like a disgruntled headmistress. "And where the actual fuck were you?" She accused, venom coating her words. She explained having a phone call from the hospital after they couldn't reach him. After they couldn't reach his wife's next of kin, they had explored her phone, trying desperately to find another family member. She relayed the fear she'd had during her journey, not knowing the details of the incident. She stated how many times she had phoned him, her frustration that she couldn't reach him, how she had phoned his office but his secretary hadn't picked up, and then like a balloon, she deflated and crumpled down onto the chair next to him to wait for the police. He was glad she had finally shut up; he didn't need to be dealing with her melodrama right now. Not when his wife was lying in a hospital bed after being violated. Not now; he had his own problems to deal with.

The Wife, the Mother, the Woman, the Victim

She was floating. Flying through a cloudless sky. She felt weightless. She had no worries. She could occasionally feel a pull at the back of her head, but it didn't bother her. She was wrapped in a soft blanket, and her nerves were numb. She felt glorious. She felt free.

The Police Officer

The police officer walked down the hospital corridor. She took some calming breaths as she saw what she assumed was the husband sitting on a chair. His head was in his hands, a typical pose for a man in this situation. He wasn't talking to the flamboyant woman who sat next to him. The police officer tried to remember the basics of her training. Sexual assault cases were day to day occurrences for her now. But to the family, this was a huge moment in their lives; it was life altering and brand new.

She spoke to the husband calmly; she explained that she would need to take a statement from his wife, that the clothes she had been wearing were now in evidence, and that officers were combing the scene.

The husband stood mute with a look of disbelief on his face, but the flamboyant woman next to him introduced herself as the victim's mother and started asking questions. Would they be able to see the victim after she woke up? Had they found any clues? The police officer nearly choked at the word clues; she hadn't thought of that word since she was a child reading Nancy Drew underneath her bedcovers with a torch when she was supposed to be sleeping. Those books were what led her to the police force. Nancy made solving crimes look so easy. The reality was much different. The reality was that nine times out of ten, the case wasn't closed, and the victim was left floating in an abyss of unanswered questions.

She reiterated the details, that the path wasn't overlooked. That nobody in the surrounding area had reported anything unusual, but they would be going door to door today to speak to the people of the local area. That the man who had phoned the ambulance hadn't seen what had happened but that they would speak to him as well, so far, no witnesses had come forward.

Next, the police officer got to the tricky part. "So far, the DNA is looking limited." Both of the victim's family members looked astounded. That was natural, as most people believed that even with a speck of DNA the case would be closed. Years of TV detective shows had given them a skewed and optimistic view of police work. She explained that investigations had shown no semen in the vagina and that further exploration had revealed that the condom hadn't been left in there.

She had very limited semen on her dress, and none had been found at the scene. Police officers were checking the vicinity and every bin in the surrounding area, but so far the condom had not been found. They might not be able to find the perpetrator, things were not looking good from an evidence perspective. All they had was a few drops of semen they were already trying to analyse and a single solitary hair that had been found tucked in the bodice of the dress.

They were hoping that the victim would be able to give a good description and that maybe, just maybe, someone would recognise the face. Maybe another woman would come forward, but only if this was part of a pattern. Only if the attacker had done this before, only if they could find him on the police database. She told the loved ones that she would do everything in her power to catch the man who had done this.

At this news, the husband excused himself, and she could hear him violently retching in the closest bathroom, and the mother of the victim slumped down in the chair with a glassy look over her face. As she walked back down the corridor, she wished she could do more. The police officer turned on her heel to go back, to try and offer some words of comfort to the family, but she saw a nurse was already there, holding the mother's hand as she cried.

The Watcher, the Waiter, the Hunter

The hunter had already taken care of some of his business. As he strode away from the scene of his crime and the bleeding women he had left behind, he had quickly formulated a short-term plan. He entered the main road and walked confidently into one of the empty cafes that lined it, the casual walk of a man with nothing to hide.

He chose the cafe for its disgusting coffee and inedible breakfasts. Very few of the town's people visited it, so it was very nearly always empty at this time. He asked the waitress for a cup of coffee and a bacon sandwich, and while she relayed this information to the cook in the kitchen, he gently removed the large clock from the wall and set it back half an hour. He carefully replaced it on the wall and surveyed it. He hoped he hadn't pushed his luck. Half an hour was a long time for a waitress to lose.

He hoped she hadn't checked the time recently, but the steaming sink and soapy glasses behind the counter gave him hope that she had been too distracted. Finally, he saw her phone lying on the counter next to the sink. It was a problem; phones were always a problem. He quickly slipped behind the counter and knocked it into the bubbling water.

He felt a small sense of power that he had turned back time. When the waitress came back from the kitchen, he was already back at his table. She subconsciously checked the time on the clock and carried on with her tasks. The watcher saw her searching the counter for her phone until she finally gave up and continued with the dishes. Then he watched as she pulled her now ruined phone from the sink, her face a picture of disbelief and horror. He smiled to himself at a job well done and settled down to read the paper whilst he waited for his sandwich.

He stayed sat there for half an hour before he visited the bathroom and flushed the condom that had been concealed in his pocket. It took more flushes than he thought it would, but he filled the toilet with balled up tissue, and eventually it disappeared. The hunter watched triumphantly as a huge piece of evidence vanished into the underground sewerage system. He smiled smugly.

After he went back to his table, he made mindless conversation with the waitress for a while, making sure he kept her back to the clock on the wall and her mind distracted. Then he requested an omelette. The waitress was shocked. The food there was terrible; customers didn't normally request seconds. In fact, they didn't normally finish what they ordered to begin with. He claimed he was still hungry after he registered her surprise, and as she went back into the kitchen, he removed the clock from the wall again and set it to the right time.

It took less time than he thought for the police to come; someone must have found the woman. He wondered who it was and how long it had taken them to find her. He wondered if she was still alive or if she was still resting on the hard ground in the position he had left her, a white sheet shielding her body from the prying eyes of the public.

He had been sat musing how he could have been so mistaken by the young woman and if maybe the waitress would be a better fit for him, when two officers came in. They questioned the waitress behind the counter if she had seen or heard anything unusual and asked him how long he had been sat. He gave them the altered time, and they confirmed it with the waitress. After they left, he breathed a huge sigh of relief, ate his omelette, and decided the waitress wasn't that pretty after all, definitely not worth his valuable time. Paid and left the establishment. He was walking on air; he felt weightless and invincible.

F.Z.CARSON

The Owners of the Terrace

The husband of the terrace was awoken by an authoritative knock on the door. He hoped it wasn't yet another door-to-door salesman who had disturbed his precious sleep or, even worse, a religious nut trying to turn him onto the path of enlightenment. He didn't need enlightenment. What he needed was enough sleep so he could do his job properly without any mistakes and without risking getting fired.

It wasn't. Instead, two uniformed police officers stood firmly on his step in their regulation boots, radios crackling from their jackets. They politely informed him that an incident had happened just outside the back of his property. "The woods?" he asked in disbelief.

The woods at the back of the property had been his and his wife's favourite part of the house when they were viewing it. They weren't really woods, just a collection of trees that had been planted long ago to shield the path. But his wife had loved that nature was just outside their back door; she persuaded him that the fact they wouldn't be overlooked made up for the small kitchen, and he agreed. Who needed an oven big enough to cook their roast turkey on Christmas day when they had trees and birds just metres from their back door? At the beginning of their lives in the terrace, they had walked the woodland path every evening, hand in hand. Regaling each other with stories from their childhoods, basking in the cool glow of the moonlight.

Gradually, things changed, and so had their working lives. Now, with him working nights and her doing mixed shifts, they were more like ships passing in the night. Occasionally sharing a quick kiss or a small dinner when their schedules collided correctly. But more often than not, he was sitting down to his breakfast while she ate her dinner. The smell of her gravy wafting across the table and putting him off his cornflakes.

The man of the terrace knew his wife was working the A and E shift right now. He hoped she hadn't seen the victim and that the small terrace that they both loved wouldn't be ruined for her.

The wife of the terrace was indeed working the A and E shift. But she hadn't been that lucky. As soon as the paramedics had relayed what had happened and where the victim had been found, she knew it was mere metres from her own home, the place where she laid her head to rest every night. She had helped cut the vibrant clothing from the young woman and placed it in the clear evidence bag for the police, a light summer dress with a ripped strap and a muddy skirt. She had administered the correct quantity of drugs into the woman's arm to help keep her calm. She had checked for evidence of rape and helped clean the wound on the back of the victim's head after the doctor had examined it.

The doctor had said the woman had been lucky. Lucky because the head wound was actually quite deep, but the woman's hair and the mud of the dirt path had managed to staunch the bleeding, so she hadn't lost too much blood. She still needed a transfusion, but it was enough of a help that she hadn't died on the path. The doctor reiterated how lucky the victim had been. The terrace nurse made a mental note to never ever use the word lucky when having a discussion about a rape victim.

She had been instructed to deal with the woman's head wound, a long and gruelling task to make sure that every single piece of dirt was obliterated from the wound. When she was happy that the wound was as sterile as she could manage, she sat for an hour and carefully stitched the woman's skin back together as neatly as she possibly could. Healing just one of the wounds that been inflicted that day.

Throughout her shift, the woman of the terrace was distracted by the victim. She kept checking on her as often as she could. She had taken coffee to the woman's husband and comforted the victim's mother when things had gotten too much. She was aware she was acting more like a family friend than a professional nurse, but she couldn't help it. The crime had happened on her doorstep. It was personal.

As her shift ended, she checked on the victim one last time. She was sitting up in bed, awake and pale, apart from the marks of the day's violation, which stood out, glaring under the artificial light.

"I hear you saved my hair," the victim stated, offering a weak smile. The nurse smiled back. She had indeed saved as much hair as she could. Other nurses would have shaved around the area for better access. But she had just trimmed the immediate area before she stitched. Then, whilst the victim was still asleep, she had braided the rest of the hair as best she could into two messy plaits so they wouldn't interfere with the wound.

She knew gently pulling apart the blood matted hair would be one of the memories that haunted her for the rest of her life. Long after she had washed the dried brown residue from under her own fingernails, she wished she could have washed it for her. To rinse away the mud and pain. To have combed it properly and offered words of comfort, like a mother to her daughter. She smiled again and said goodbye. She wouldn't forget this night.

The woman of the terrace left the hospital and started the drive home. She wanted to call her husband, but as she checked the time on the dashboard, she realised it was too late; he would have started work already, and she didn't want to disturb him. She didn't want to worry him. She pulled into the parking space outside of her house and shivered, thinking about how a crime had taken place metres away from the bedroom she slept in. She didn't want to go into the house; she didn't want to spend the night alone.

As she shut off the engine, she saw the front door open. There her husband stood, a pool of light from the hallway surrounding him, illuminating him like an angel. Clearly, he had heard the news and called into work with a family emergency so she wouldn't have to be alone. So she wouldn't have to sleep alone. Later, when she sat on the sofa, drinking the hot, sweet milky tea her husband had made her, she could hear him double checking that the doors and windows were locked. She also noticed a new camera had been fitted onto the back wall of the house, watching the path below. And the bedroom window was open again.

The Son

Mummy hadn't picked him up from school, nor had daddy or even grandma. Instead, he was walking back home with his quiet, reserved grandad. They couldn't take the woodland path tonight because it was taped off and there were lots of police men.

Inwardly, the little boy corrected himself, not police men, police officers. Mummy had driven this thought into his mind. "Anyone can be anything. No matter if they are a girl or a boy." She had laughed whilst correcting the words in one of his picture books with a big black pen. Daddy said mummy was a crazy feminist, and he was angry that she had drawn all over one of his books, but the son thought mummy made a lot of sense.

Grandad wasn't saying a lot; he didn't normally say much, preferring instead to let grandma do the talking. Grandma did lots of talking, just like mummy. When they got together it was a hurricane of words. A tidal wave of laughter washing over everyone who sat near them. Whilst his grandad would sit quietly in the corner, watching it like a west end production, and his daddy would sit awkwardly wincing and tutting as the two women got louder and louder as they talked faster and faster.

The son liked it when his mummy and grandma got together; they spoke with their voices, their faces, and their arms. They laughed, interrupted, and jumped from one topic to another without pause. Watching and listening to them was fun.

Where was grandma? She and grandad were always together, joined at the hip, peas in a pod. A very old, wrinkly pod. The son hoped she was okay; she was getting older and wrinkles were beginning to line her face. But then his mind turned to more important things. What if mummy didn't get home soon? What if daddy had to work late again? Who on earth would make his tea? Who would look after him?

His grandad answered his first question by ordering pizza, very unusual for grandad. He struggled phoning the order in, as if a lifetime of watching his wife speak had made him forget how to use his own words. They watched one of the films mummy had left strewn about the side, and his granddad put him to bed. The son didn't do his reading that night but only remembered it later, when he was in bed. He had crept down the stairs to tell his grandad that he must do his reading; otherwise his teacher would be upset, and that after, grandad must write it in his school book. But instead, he caught his grandfather crying on the sofa.

The son felt a waft of sympathy for this old man, who sat alone on a sofa that was not his own, without the anchor of his wife. He crawled into his grandad's lap and suggested that maybe, just maybe, they could sit together and watch another film until he fell asleep. His grandad agreed, and they fell asleep together on the sofa, the women of their lives absent.

The Wife, the Mother, the Woman, the Victim

The police officer had been really nice; she had explained what was happening and then what was going to happen, all whilst the victim had sat quietly in bed, trying not to cry or scream. Trying to stop her body from curling up into itself with rage and shame. The officer asked if she knew her attacker, and the woman said she didn't think so. She'd racked her brains for a long time, wondering if she would be able to place his face, but nothing had come to her. Surely, he wasn't just a random stranger. Normal people didn't do the things he had done to her, to people they didn't know. She had been asked to describe him; "big and bearded" was all she could think of. She couldn't remember the details of his face or the colour of his eyes. She hadn't seen enough of his skin to know if he had any visible scars or tattoos. Distinguishing features the police officer had called them.

She felt useless; she could only recall stupid things, the smell of artificial tomato on his breath, the glove that she had bitten as she tried to force him off, the way the acrylic wool had squeaked against her teeth, and the fact that his shirt collar was stained with sweat.

She had explained the attack in detail while the officer had videoed her. Re-living the moments from when she said goodbye to the old man to when she had been saved by the man in a suit. The two good men who had bookended her story, whilst one villainous one rested in between. A thorn between two roses.

The police officer had comforted her, tilting her head to one side in sympathy and nodding at the right moments, and she had reassured her they were looking. They would always be looking for her attacker. She gave the names of organisations that provided help for women like her, organisations that could listen to her fears, and groups where she could hear other women relive their own experiences. Then the police officer had provided her with a bag of new clothes. Her own had been taken as evidence. Grey jogger bottoms and a spice girl's t-shirt. Clearly, they were clothes that had been donated long after girl power had fallen from fashion, items that she would never normally wear.

She thought about asking after her dress. It was vintage, a family heirloom that had been handed down from her grandmother. She had loved that dress. Her grandfather had proposed to her grandmother whilst she wore the dress. He'd brought the fabric too, on a far-off tropical island during his army service. He had given it to her nan as a gift when they were young and courting, she had sewn it up on the old treadle sewing machine that now sat in the corner of the wife's living room. Another family heirloom passed down. The dress had happy memories woven into the very threads of the fabric. Now it was covered in her blood and a nameless man's fluid, resting in a clear plastic bag, ready to be looked at under a microscope. Now it was ruined. She decided not to ask; she never wanted to see that dress again.

The Husband

The husband wondered if his wife would be angry. He had feared walking into the room after the police officer had left with her notebook full of statements and descriptions. But his wife was pleased to see him; she had cried exhausted tears all over the grey trousers they had provided her.

He realised this was the first time he had ever seen his wife look casual. Even her lounging about clothes were silk pyjamas in tropical colours. Her robe was Chinese inspired, a ferocious tiger jumping from the red silk in colourful embroidery.

The last time he had seen his wife look anything less than perfect, she had just spent eight hours labouring to give him his son. She had been covered in sweat, blood, and other disgusting mementos of birth, but she had looked wonderful. She had crooned at their son's face and commented on the beauty of his perfectly formed limbs while the doctors had stitched her down below. She had been a vision of motherhood. Cradling a small baby, whispering that she would love him. She was instantly infatuated. The husband had been more than a little jealous.

But now she just looked tired and broken. The doctor had offered to discharge her. He thought the best place for her would be at home, surrounded by those she loved and wrapped in a blanket of familiarity.

But the husband was smarter; he knew his wife. He knew how fragile she was, how needy. This would break her; she would be a shell of a human. And what about him? How would he explain this to his own family? To his colleagues at work. Would it be in the papers? Splashed across the 6 o'clock news. Would the whole of England know his wife had been raped? Talking behind his back.

At that moment, his assistant came into his mind, and he wanted to run away. This wasn't what he wanted; once again, his wife had let the chaos of her life interfere with his, and nothing would be the same again.

After the Incident - Part One

Big moments in our lives can upset our patterns. A cup of coffee with a friend is cancelled when they move out of town. Roast dinner with Grandma is void after she dies. A near miss on a roundabout can scare you into never using that road again. Some people cope well with the new changes in their lives; it helps them feel safe again. For others, they will struggle every day wishing things were how they were before.

The Son

Everyone was being weird. He had woken up in his own bed, obviously carried there by some unknown force, and Daddy was home. Daddy was never home on weekdays, not unless he had a holiday booked off work, and even then, Daddy never took him to school, preferring instead to stay in bed and make the most of his time off. But this morning, Daddy had actually woken him up and supervised his dressing; he didn't tuck his top in like Mummy did, and he didn't say he looked smart.

Daddy made breakfast too, fumbling about with the toaster and boiling the kettle. He struggled to find the plates in the cupboard. The little boy wasn't surprised; he had never seen Daddy in the kitchen cooking why would he know where the plates were kept. But most importantly, Daddy had put Nutella on his toast; it wasn't Friday. The chocolate spread was for Fridays only; something very strange was happening.

Granddad was still there as well, stood in the corner of the kitchen, drinking coffee and not speaking. He still looked very tired. He wasn't looking at Daddy, but occasionally shot a small smile at the son. Daddy was ignoring Granddad, the son wondered if daddy had been angry that granddad had let him stay up to watch extra films, and that's why they weren't speaking.

Daddy believed in strict bedtimes. In routine. Especially when that routine was for children.

He wondered if he should own up and explain to his father that the extra films were his idea. That he had just wanted to cheer granddad up and sit with him so he wouldn't be alone. So he wouldn't have to cry alone.

Granddad wasn't alone now. He knew grandma was in the house somewhere; her coat was thrown over the banister. They had a set of hooks by the door, but grandma didn't use those. Instead, she spread her things wherever she wanted with the same chaos his mother did. He could smell grandmas' perfume as well; it was rich and throaty. It made him think of dark places and smoky rooms. It was very different from the vanilla smell his mummy wore; she smelled like cupcakes.

Finally, he knew it was time to have his questions answered. Daddy never took him to school, and grandma and granddad never had sleepovers. Not even after mummy's birthday parties, daddy would always phone them a taxi, even if the sun was already coming up. Mummy always let the son stay up for her birthday parties; the house was full of people like mummy on those nights, colourful people.

Grownups would be reciting poetry in the kitchen while somebody strummed an acoustic guitar in the garden. Mummy and grandma ruled those parties floating from room to room, discussing everything from art to politics, whilst granddad fiddled with the record player, taking requests for jazz and 80's rock. Daddy always stood in the corner, drinking Irish whiskey looking uncomfortable surrounded by the flamboyance of his wife's friends, occasionally chatting with a plus one who was in the tech industry. Daddy hated the parties. It was the only occasion he allowed mummy's friends in the house.

He cleared his throat, not wanting to break the silence of the kitchen. "Where's my mummy?" His father immediately turned away and started busying himself with adding water to the coffee maker. "She's not well" and that was it. Mummy was apparently "not well." The son thought this was highly unlikely. Mummy had been poorly lots of times, but she had still taken him to school. Even that time she had a sickness bug and had thrown up on the woodland path. She always took him to school. He went to ask another question, wanting to know exactly how mummy was sick because maybe he had it too.

They had been poorly together once before, and it had been quite lovely. Between fits of coughing, mummy had read him a big boy book called The Hobbit. She had done the voices of the characters, always spluttering and coughing after she did the deep voice of the wizard. They had wrapped themselves in the big blanket grandma had crocheted a long time ago from scraps of wool and drank cups of honey and lemon. For a few days, they had lived in their own little world, and it was perfect. Daddy had stayed away from them and slept in the spare room; he didn't want to get sick.

He decided that if mummy was ill, then he would be too, so he could stay home from school and daddy could go back to work where he belonged. He opened his mouth to tell his father. "Shoes on, it's time for school." The stern quality of his father's voice made him realise that daddy was home for a reason, and he wasn't happy about it. The son decided a day at school might be easier than a day with his father, so he went and put his small feet in his shoes. Before he could worry about how he would tie his shoelaces without his mummy's help, his granddad was bent down doing them for him. "Can granddad come too?" turned out to be the last question the son would ask his father that morning.

The Teacher

The teaching assistant poked her head around the door and informed the teacher that a parent was waiting in reception and wanted to talk to her. Bugger, she thought to herself. She was only halfway down her coffee and had been idly staring out of the classroom window, looking at the parents' milling about the playground.

The teacher wondered which parent it was, probably one of the ones who thought their little darling was far more intelligent than they actually were. She was always fielding suggestions from helicopter parents on how to improve her teaching, how so and so should really go up a reading group, how what's his name wasn't actually a naughty boy; it might actually be the child he was sitting next to, maybe they were the bad influence.

Parents in this day and age had too much time on their hands and too much access to other nutcase parents on the internet who agree with their views. Recently, a parent had informed her that they were no longer using the word "no" in front of their child, and they didn't want the teacher to use it either. Apparently, the word was knocking his self-esteem; he needed things explaining to him carefully and quietly, and he should be able to express his emotions by screaming and punching if he wanted to. The teacher had openly scoffed and told the parent that she was one of seven children and that her mother had used the word "no" so often that she and all her siblings answered to it. Naturally, the parent had complained about her attitude, and she had received the first ever warning of her teaching career from the new head teacher.

She put her coffee cup on the side and ambled down the hall, passing finger paintings and poetry, wondering what crackpot idea was being pushed by a parent this time; she'd have to tread carefully. Another warning meant another uncomfortable hour in the head teacher's office after school whilst he suggested ways she could "improve". Courses she could take, books she could read, and she was much too old for that shit.

Stood in reception was an impeccably dressed man. He had the sort of neatness you only see in magazines and looked like an advertisement for the local golf club; A prestigious, pompous place she had tried to avoid. Next to him stood a small boy from her class, the son of the colourful mother. This was his father. She vaguely remembered him from the reception open evening she had hosted; he had been on his phone while she was speaking and had shown no interest in the creative subjects the children would be taking part in, only asking about maths, writing, and reading. She had thought him rather rude. And even at the time, she had noted the stark contrast between the boys two parents. One was curves and softness, the other was all hard angles.

Standing a little way behind him was an elderly gentleman she didn't know. He had a steady hand resting on the child's shoulder like an anchor. Was he keeping the child upright, or was the child keeping him upright? The teacher mused to herself.

The father looked uncomfortable and motioned to the child next to him pointedly. Clearly, this wasn't a conversation for small ears. The teacher asked the receptionist to take him to the classroom and get him settled in. The father didn't acknowledge his son leaving at first, but after the elderly gentleman had squeezed the child to him with a big bear hug, he had clearly decided he couldn't be outdone and had also hugged his child.

Years of working with children meant the teacher could read them like books. She could identify a loving parent from ten yards and an absent one from twenty. The hug between the child and the man she now assumed was his grandfather had been caring, if a little restrained, like two new friends who weren't quite sure if they should hug or not, if such an intimate gesture might frighten the other off. The embrace between the father and son was just plain awkward. Clearly, it didn't happen very often. Afterwards, the father had checked his shirt for wrinkles, without a glance towards the direction his son had just walked with the teaching assistant.

The father started talking as soon as his son had gone from view. His voice was hushed to almost a whisper, as though he were sharing some terrible secret. There had been an incident. The child didn't know what had happened, but he knew something was going on. He would be bringing the child to school for a few days, but he didn't know how long; he was a busy man and he needed to get back to work. Would it be possible to put the child in before and after school club? The teacher stood waiting. "An incident?" she questioned, looking back and forth between the father and the elderly gentleman.

The father looked uncomfortable again, and he saw the corners of his mouth tighten in restraint. It's a family matter, he responded looking to the side. A lie. The teacher started a prepared speech about child wellbeing and how she needed to look after the small boy's mental health as well as his educational needs. Really, she could do with the facts. But more importantly, her curiosity had been peaked; she could see now that the boy's parents really were an odd pairing, like a beige wall teamed with colourful graffiti. Had they separated? Was that the incident to which the father referred?

The grandfather interrupted her "His mother was raped yesterday, after she dropped him off at school, and he won't be going to school club. I'll pick him up myself if his father's too busy". The teacher gasped not only because of the news of the rape but also because the two men who stood before her were clearly at odds.

As the grandfather's words sank in, she was hit with the sudden realisation that this had never happened before. In the whole of her teaching career, this had never happened, and she had no idea how to deal with it, and she was fairly sure that none of the head teachers suggested reading materials would cover it either. She had comforted children through countless divorces, deaths of family members, and even a still born baby sister who exited the womb prematurely but perfectly formed at seven months. But never had a mother been raped. She was speechless.

She felt a cold shiver run down her body. Rape was every woman's fear. Rape was what made women cross the street, pay extortionate amounts for car parks with good lighting, and keep their keys in their hands when it was dark and they were walking home. Rape made women coiled springs ready to attack at any moment, and it had happened in this town, near this school, just minutes after she had seen the woman with her very own eyes. Just moments after she had waved to her.

The teacher assured the father that she would do everything she could to make sure the child was okay, but even as she spoke, she could feel herself stumbling over the words with shock. Then she looked back and forth between the two men and said the only other thing she could think of, "I'm sorry".

The Incident

As she went back to the classroom, her legs felt like lead. She needed to sit down to come up with a plan for dealing with this. Should she warn the other mothers? Should she speak to the small boy? Hopefully, he was blind to the truth. Hopefully, as soon as the classroom filled with children, his mind would be so occupied that he would forget whatever horrors were happening at home.

As she entered, she saw the small boy was sat in the reading corner, not really looking at the book in his hands. It was written all over his face that he knew something was wrong. So, she went to her desk and pulled out one of her emergency biscuits. One of the ones with chocolate that she hid from the teaching assistant. She sat with the small boy whilst he ate the biscuit, drinking the cold coffee that felt as bitter as her soul.

F.Z.CARSON

The Old Man

The old man had heard the school bell ten minutes ago. Normally, the young woman was here already. He had decided today was the day to offer her a cup of tea, but he had changed his plan. Instead of inviting the young woman in, he had pulled two peeling iron chairs from his shed and a wrought iron table. He would offer her a drink outside; that way, she might feel more comfortable than going into his house.

He had been preparing all morning; he had hoisted himself onto a stool and stiffly pulled his late wife's floral tea set out of the cupboard, then washed it carefully. She had loved this tea set. He had given it to her as a gift for their twenty-fifth wedding anniversary, and she used it all the time. "It's too beautiful to stay in a cupboard".

He ran an arthritis-ridden finger down a crack in the sugar bowl and admired how neatly he had reattached the handle to the milk jug. It was well used, but still beautiful. He popped his hand on the side of the teapot, making sure it was still warm, and continued to wait. He wondered if he should try and dig the old knitted tea cosy out of the cupboard. It was threadbare and stained, but at least it would help to keep the pot warm. He decided against it; he might miss her while he fumbled about inside. She might walk past as he tried to coax his body into bending towards the cupboards and stretching in search of the cosy.

The old man's nervous fingers picked at the peeling paint of the table. His wife had chosen this set. We can sit in the garden and pretend we're French she exclaimed! This wasn't the France he remembered; his France was full of blown-off body parts and mud, loud shouts over gunfire, and praying that he would get home in one piece so he could see his sweetheart once again.

He spun his wedding ring around and tried to ignore how loose it felt and how the only thing keeping it on was the wrinkles of his fingers. The woman was very late now. Maybe the little boy was poorly; there had been a chill in the air recently; hopefully he hadn't come down with a cold. A tall man and an elderly gentleman were beginning to walk past. They weren't speaking to each other. The old man offered a "good morning" out into the air. The elderly gentleman replied in kind, but the younger man continued walking. The old man noticed that the tall man was walking slightly faster than the elderly gentleman, almost two strides ahead of him. The faster pace made him wonder if they were actually walking together. Or if they were actually strangers.

The old man waited for another half an hour. Clearly, she wasn't coming. He tried to hide his disappointment at the missed interaction but decided to look on the bright side. He would have time to repaint the table; his late wife would be horrified that he had let it get into this condition. He'd go to the hardware store today and pick out some new paint. If he was quick he might have it done by the evening and then it would be ready for tomorrow.

F.Z.CARSON

The Husband

Why wouldn't his bloody in-laws fucking leave? He was sick of them being there, in his house, judging him, judging the way he had handled the situation. His mother-in-law had actually used his room last night and slept in the same bed as his wife, holding her hand and stroking her hair. Part of him was relieved that his mother-in-law had taken the night shift. Whatever they had given his wife at the hospital had worn off, and she had spent a good deal of time sweating and shaking in her sleep. When she was actually asleep. When she was awake, she cried, and he could hear her from the sanctuary of the spare room.

He had gone in to see her in the morning to see if she was in any condition to walk their child to school and had nearly retched at the smell of her. The blood in her hair smelled like burnt copper, and small flecks of it had landed on her pillowcase in the night, staining it like cinnamon. He could see sweat patches through her t-shirt, and her skin was covered in a sheen of oil.

His mother-in-law had rolled over and glared at him. "What are you doing?" she had hissed angrily. He replied that it was time to take their son to school, and he thought a walk might do his wife good. His mother-in-law called him an ignorant bastard and ordered him out of the room.

His father-in-law was no easier to get along with. He said nothing and offered no words of condolence. He had slept on the sofa. Only waking to help carry his daughter to bed, and now he stood in the husband's kitchen drinking yet another cup of coffee.

He could hear his mother-in-law talking in soothing tones upstairs, and then he could hear the thud, thud, thud of her coming downstairs. The woman refused to use a stick, instead banging about wherever she went as she manoeuvred the mass of her ageing body and tried with great difficulty to keep it upright.

He turned to face the kitchen door, ready to politely but firmly broach the subject of their leaving. He didn't have a chance to ask; a cup of tea for his wife was his mother in laws suggestion. At this rate, he'd have to start fitting shopping into his day as well, especially considering his father-in-law was working his way through more cups of coffee than he had ever seen a human drink. Surely by now he should be a jittering wreck, but instead he stood as calmly and quietly as ever. Like a stone statue or one of those painted street performers he had seen in Covent Garden.

The husband opened a cupboard door and found glasses. Awkwardly, he fumbled around the kitchen, trying to find mugs and tea bags. There was no system to the kitchen; his wife had haphazardly thrown things in the cupboards. He found two boxes of tea bags, one marked decaf. Shit, which did his wife have? He didn't drink decaf, so surely those were hers, but there was green tea in the cupboard too, and he distinctly remembered his wife saying that green tea tasted like cat piss, so maybe both of them were for guests. His wife, unlike him, liked to be as hospitable as possible.

He was fumbling over his decision when his mother-in-law piped up that she'd have one as well, decaf. He breathed a sigh of relief; the decaf must be there for her. Trust his wife to cater for his mother in law's whims. Next, he picked up the sugar and looked at his mother-in-law, she shook her head. What about his wife? He took his tea with one sugar, but did she? He threw two spoonful's in the cup whilst his mother-in-law raised her eyebrows, then he threw in two more. Sugar for shock they said. It was basically medicine; it didn't matter if she normally had it.

It never occurred to the husband to be embarrassed that he didn't know how his own wife took her tea.

The Wife, the Mother, the Woman, the Victim

Her head hurt. Jesus Christ, her cunt hurt. It throbbed, reminding her of what had happened. Her night had been very fitful. Her mother had slept beside her, cradling her like a baby when she could bear to be touched and speaking soothing words from arm's length when she couldn't. It was a relief to have her mother lie next to her; she hadn't wanted her husband beside her. To feel the scratching of his hair in the night and to see his morning erection stood proud as soon as she woke up. She wanted to steer clear of that area for a while. Sex was ruined.

She sat up in bed and looked down at herself. She didn't want to see her body; it didn't feel like hers now. It felt dirty and ruined. She needed a shower.

She went to walk to the bathroom when her husband came in; he was brandishing a cup of tea in front of him like he was giving her all the gold in the world. He looked proud and a little smug with himself for achieving such a monumental task. She thanked him and tried to force a smile. He was beginning to make small talk, telling her that he had taken their son to school, that the police had called and there was no update, that work had given him two weeks off to deal with what had happened, but that he was hoping to be back in one. There was a big project coming up, and he didn't want to miss out. How typical of her husband, he was already thinking about damage control.

Then he started complaining that her parents were still here. Her mother had taken his bed last night; he had been relegated to the spare room, he was annoyed by their attitudes, they blamed him for not getting there quicker, he had been busy, and her father had nearly drunk all the coffee.

The wife interrupted his stream of moaning; she didn't want to hear this right now. "I want a shower," she stated in a matter of fact way. He replied that she couldn't get her stitches wet yet. "Then I'll have a bath," she responded. She was sick of his bullshit. She knew why he hadn't answered his phone. She'd known for months and had ignored it. Of course her mother had stayed; she had been attacked, she had been raped!

He hadn't even asked if she was okay. She grabbed the cup of tea from his hand and took it to the bathroom. She started the hot water and waited for the steam to rise. She didn't need cold water today; she wanted it boiling to eradicate every trace of the man who had hurt her. She took a sip of tea, it was vile. Filled to the brim with sugar, it was sickly sweet and heavy. She threw it down the toilet and flushed.

She sat down in the bath, ignoring the burning of her skin. The victim grabbed a loofah from the side and systematically began to scrub her body from neck to toe. She still didn't feel clean. There was dirt under her finger nails; she attacked them with a nail brush. The hard bristles felt good, so she used them on her body next. She wished she could wash her hair it felt disgusting. But she couldn't risk her stitches, so instead she took a pair of nail scissors and sawed off the long plaits the nurse had made for her with such care. Instantly, her head felt lighter. She dropped them on the floor. A dried mass of blood, mud, and hair on the bathmat. She wished she could cut off her skin and take it away as easily as she had her hair. Peel away the layer of flesh that the vile man had touched.

She began on her body again. Adding layers of soap and refreshing the boiling water. Scouring her skin again and again, just trying to rid herself of the hunter's essence, she was sure she could still smell him and could still taste artificial tomatoes in her mouth. She grabbed her toothbrush from the side and brushed until her gums were raw and bleeding, then she went back to her skin again. By this point it was blossoming patches of red colour. Small amounts of blood threaded their way into the bath water. She washed her vagina as best she could without screaming. It didn't even feel right when she touched it, like it was no longer attached to her own body. It felt like one of those rubber chickens you find in a joke shop, artificial and comical.

She was desperately crying in the bath. Noisy sobs coming out of her like a child. She couldn't get clean.

The Husband

His wife had gotten into the bath, and he had gone back downstairs to try and approach the idea of his in-laws leaving again. She had been upstairs for ten minutes when they heard thrashing around in the tub and violent sobbing. His mother-in-law was up before he was, taking the stairs as fast as her varicose veined legs would carry her. He took them three at a time, knocking his mother-in-law into a wall to make sure he won the race, overtaking her halfway up.

He tried to open the bathroom door but faltered. It was locked. How in hell would he open it? He couldn't play the hero if he couldn't reach his wife. The answer came from his father-in-law who didn't hesitate and threw his entire body weight against the door, ripping it from his frame.

The three of them stopped dead, looking into the room. They all saw his wife. She was sitting, surrounded by pinkish-red bathwater, holding a nail brush and sobbing. The husband faltered again as he looked at his wife's torn skin, red grazes blooming over the dark bruises of the previous day. Yet again, he thought about his mistress, about her smooth skin, uniform in colour and texture.

As his in-laws gently took the scrubbing brush from his wife's hands and wrapped her in a towel, his thoughts were only with his mistress. He needed to call her. He needed to explain.

The Mother, the Grandmother, the Wife, the Mother in Law

The mother of the victim sat at her daughter's kitchen table with her husband. His head was in his hands. Her son in law had left for a "walk" after the incident in the bathroom. Yet again, he had left her daughter to flounder and cope alone.

"What do we do now?" She questioned her husband. She didn't expect a response from a man of so few words. Unexpectedly, the man she loved lifted his head from his hands and began to speak.

The Man in the Suit

The man in the suit stood in his back garden. He had been sent home from work and given the rest of the week off. The police had been earlier and had taken his statement. The suit he had been wearing the previous day had been stored in a carrier bag in case they needed it for evidence. They didn't; he'd had to prove where he had been. Luckily, he had clocked in at work, and several people had seen him run out of the building on his quest for cash. He wasn't a suspect now; they didn't need his suit.

He put it in a wheelbarrow in the garden, along with his vomit-stained shoes. The blood had dried on the suit jacket like tie dye, rust colour had worked its way into the fibres. Dry cleaning would be of no use, and he was absolutely sure he never wanted to wear it again. He doused it in vodka and took a swig from the bottle. The hours after the incident had been a mixture of drinking and bad dreams. He'd reached the point now where his body craved the release of alcohol more than it craved water.

He looked awful. His pregnant co-worker had phoned him twice and he hadn't picked up, so this morning she had arrived at his house. She looked different out of her work clothes. She was wearing a floral wrap dress that accentuated her large baby bump. He felt guilty that she had come to see him, especially after he had ruined her leaving do. She had made him drink water and told him to pull himself together.

He told her how helpless he felt. How he couldn't get the vision of the woman out of his head. He told her of his disappointment in his mother cheating on his father and how it had affected his trust in women. He told her about his philandering ways and how he didn't even know the name of the woman who had stolen her money. He told her all of his sins. Confessing them like a killer in a church.

And she laughed. She told him he was no different than thousands of men on the planet, apart from that now he knew he wanted to do better. Then she left; she had been having Braxton hicks all morning and was starting to get tired.

That's when he had taken the suit to the garden and thrown it in the wheelbarrow. He needed it gone. He lit a cigarette and then set alight the messy fabric; it started to burn almost instantly, the vodka feeding the fire like it had fed him over the past hours.

He watched it until it became a smouldering mass of charcoal. Then he went into his kitchen, poured the rest of the alcohol down the sink, laced up his trainers, and started to run.

He ran like a man possessed, trying only to concentrate on the sound of his feet hitting the pavement. He didn't pay attention to where he was going or how long he had been running. Twice he threw up at the side of the road, a combination of dehydration from excess alcohol and physical exertion making his stomach heave. The muscles of his legs stretched and moaned as he took each step.

He had hoped the fire would cleanse him and that running would help him forget. But it was still there; he could see the blood dripping down her thigh, fear in her eyes, and he could smell the wound on the back of her head and the scents of the earth that had surrounded them. He threw up again and laid on the floor. He had subconsciously ended up on the woodland path.

He looked around; any traces of the crime were gone. The area had been searched and searched again by the police. He wondered what they had found. If anything. Even the blood on the ground had been washed away by a night's worth of rain. It made him angry. Why did it look so clean? How was there no trace of the hideous crime that had been committed?

His phone pinged. A picture of a baby girl popped up, "Born at 6.45 p.m., 8 lbs and 6 ounces, mum and baby both well." He quickly texted back; no wonder his co-worker had looked uncomfortable; she must have been silently labouring while he went through a list of his faults. He texted his congratulations and asked for the name. He received a single word answer "Hope".

At that moment he understood why the fire couldn't cleanse him and why the running couldn't clear his mind. He couldn't forget this; he couldn't ignore it and continue with his previous life, he needed to make a difference, to be the change. He needed hope. He stood back up and began to run home.

The Old Man

He hadn't seen the woman for the rest of the week. The table and chairs lay waiting at the front of the house, clean and freshly painted. He was miserable. His son hadn't been in touch aside from his Wednesday phone call, and he was lonely.

He considered trying to make a new connection, thumbing through a bunch of leaflets a kindly church goer had left one day. Choirs, lunch clubs, book clubs the thought of them all made him feel deflated. He was useless in social situations without his wife; she had held the conversations for both of them, and she always knew what to say.

He swept the leaflets into the bin. He picked up the phone and tried to phone his son. His son offered a tone of surprise at his father ringing him on the weekend; he wanted to know what was wrong. Was he okay? He replied that he was okay, but he just wanted to check in. The old man was hoping for an offer of a visit, a chance to reminisce with someone who had known his wife as well, a friendly connection of some sort; surely this was the least his son could do. After all, he had helped to create him, raise him, his blood ran through his sons' veins. Instead, he was being met with a stunted silence, he could hear the high-pitched tones of a woman in the background, a siren who was clearly trying to coax his son back to bed.

His son said nothing, and in a moment of blinding rage, the old man hung up the phone and ripped the cord from the wall.

He detached himself from the world.

F.Z.CARSON

The Husband

The husband sat in the local supermarket car park, waiting for his mistress to arrive. He had left his wife and child at home, watching cartoons under a blanket on the sofa. He noted angrily that the child was the only one who could touch his wife now without her cringing. She openly shuddered at his touch and laid on the edge of their bed at night, careful to make sure their bodies didn't touch. Sometimes in the morning, when he awoke, she was already up and gone. This was an uncommon occurrence for a woman who loved staying in bed. In the beginning of their relationship, the bed had been their base camp; it was where they ate, slept, and fucked. But then, over time, they found other responsibilities; shopping that needed to be done, chores to do, and guests to entertain. Like his bloody in-laws.

He had finally dispatched them a few days before, making excuses about needing to care for his wife, that she was relying on them too much, and that they needed the space to be a family again. So they could get back to normal.

But really, he just wanted them out of the house; he needed room to breathe, room to phone his mistress, and room to ignore the crying of his wife when their son was in bed.

Plus, he was jealous. The first time he had heard his wife laugh since the incident was because her mother had been dancing in the kitchen. It had been a sharp laugh, the kind someone makes when they feel as though all of the laughter has been sucked out of the world and they are surprised at themselves. His son had formed an unlikely friendship with his grandfather building Lego and playing cars. His son did the talking while the grandfather nodded, glad again to have someone to speak for him whilst his wife was preoccupied. It had been a struggle to make them leave, and they still visited most days, but at least he could breathe at night.

If anything, his wife had deflated again since they'd left. Her hair still wasn't brushed, and the brutal haircut she had given herself now stuck up at odd angles. She wasn't wearing her usual clothes, but she wasn't wearing the clothes he had brought her either. A muted palette of pale colours and simple cuts purchased from designer boutiques hung in her wardrobe untouched. Instead, she wore pyjamas. Christmas print and flannel, worn with the same dressing gown she had worn when their son was born. Her Chinese kimono was thrown carelessly on the floor, ignored.

He drummed his fingers on the wheel and looked at his watch. He'd been gone for half an hour. After a few days of apologies and pleading texts, he had managed to get his secretary to phone him back. She had gathered what had happened immediately; it had been spread across the papers and around the office. The local news had run a feature on it, giving as many details as they could manage. The town gym now offered self-defence lessons for women; everyone was exploiting his situation.

His boss had phoned and given him leave, he hadn't mentioned the secretary, only offering him as much time as he needed to care for his wife. The husband had replied that two weeks should be enough and that he would still be available to work from home. He didn't need or want to stop working, he might even be back early.

His secretary walked across the car park and let herself into the car, sitting primly on the passenger seat. She looked amazing, clean, and well-tailored, wearing the sombre, muted tones he liked, and her long hair was flowing down her back like a silky rope. He hugged her immediately and began his apology. He was sorry this had happened; he had ruined things between them. His wife's incident had ruined everything they had.

His mistress fell into his arms, immediately falling for his lies. He wanted a life with her, something uncomplicated. He assured her that it might take longer because of his wife's situation, but that he wanted to be with her. Would she wait for him? Would she love him? He needed her; she was his port in the storm of his wife and the incident she had brought into their lives.

The secretary was young and naive; she believed all of the lies, and she had been pleased by the attention she had received from her boss. She had wanted a fling at first, but he seemed so stable and reliable, his wife was obviously not deserving of him or the life he provided. He had talked in length about how slovenly she was and how she always drew attention to herself.

Secretly, the mistress wondered if the wife had been having an affair of her own, one that had gone sour. With one of the delinquents that her lover said were his wife's friends, one of the dirty artists who came to the house once a year for a party. Maybe one of those people was responsible for the so called rape. She relayed the idea to the husband and tightened her grasp on him once again.

The Wife, the Mother, the Woman, the Victim

The victim had just fielded yet another call from the counsellor who was trying to meet with her. She had wanted to avoid the conversation, but her husband's eyes were everywhere. He had already accused her of not wanting to get better. Like she had an infection and was refusing to take her medicine. This wasn't an infection that drugs could fix; this was much bigger. The thought of what had happened was a flesh-eating parasite working from the centre of her body outward. She couldn't stop it; no one could stop it. There was no cure.

She didn't watch the news anymore. Not since she had seen the photo fit that a police sketch artist had provided. It had amazed her that during her interview, the artist had seemed to relish the small details she was able to provide. The open pores on the man's nose, the coarseness of his beard, he had taken a look at the bite mark on her neck and gauged with a creative eye how big to draw the mouth. He had used imagination and artistic licence and had succeeded in creating an image that made her blood run cold and her skin crawl.

She turned her head to face the small child snuggled beside her. He was deep in slumber on the sofa while her husband shopped for supplies. She could describe her son in detail without even looking, the long silver scar on his knee from when he came off his bike, the perfect roundness of the back of his head, the exact colour and shade of his eyes, how they looked like the deep blue ocean an ex-boyfriend had once taken her to see. Not empty and dark but full of life, of a world beneath the surface. Her ex had awoken her early and dragged her half-asleep body onto a boat so she could see the sea just after the sun had risen, a sparkling blue diamond that stretched across the horizon, crowned by a ball of fire.

Right now, her son was sound asleep, sucking his thumb like he did when he was small. She gently pulled his thumb from his mouth; her husband hated thumb sucking and called him a baby when he did it, quoting statistics about misshapen teeth and speech impediments. But she knew it was a source of comfort that he needed right now. He wasn't sleeping well; you could hear him tossing and turning in bed at night, aware that something had altered his world but not sure what. Very often, she went into his room at night and crawled into the single bed with him, cocooning his body with her own like a blanket, relieved to have an excuse not to share with her husband.

She stood up slowly, taking care not to wake her child, and moved across the room to go upstairs. She wanted to take a look at herself. She had always scoffed when male writers described women looking at their bodies in the mirror, saying that real women didn't admire their breasts or their hips. But here she was, a pile of her clothes at her feet, looking. Examining, not admiring.

She started with her feet; there was no evidence of the vile hunters attacking there, just her own. The scrubbing in the bath had resulted in patches of unsightly scabs forming across the more delicate areas of her skin. Next, she looked at the midsection; she had faint bruising along her hips where he had lain on top of her, pressing his body into her small frame, and bruises had appeared on her legs where she had thrashed against the ground, trying to escape.

She couldn't bear to look at her vagina; a space that had once been so sacred no longer felt like a temple but more like a well-trodden path in a farmer's field. It should have been private, but it wasn't. She understood now why farmers brandished guns at trespassers.

Her arms were black and purple and bore more signs of her attack on herself. Her breasts were seemingly unscathed by the rape but had taken a beating from her self-deprecation as well.

The bite mark on her neck was yellow and black, glaring against the white of her skin. It didn't look anything like the hickeys she had been given as a teenager. These had been worn as a badge of honour, of a passion she had shared with some boy. She remembered girls in her classes pretending to be embarrassed when they were pointed out but never making a move to cover them up.

Her hair was again a result of her rage. It was short and choppy and still needed washing. She thought mentally about how many more days until she should do it. Then she'd have to go to the hairdressers and have it sorted out. Her hairdresser would be horrified; she didn't even like it when the woman cut her own split ends, tutting about unevenness and blunt edges. She'd have to tell them why she hacked it off. Presumably they already knew; the salon stocked a range of newspapers as well as fashion magazines. The rape had been reported along with the man they were looking for; so far, the woman hadn't been named. A small privilege for the victim.

She wondered how she would manage at the salon. She hadn't been out of the house since the attack, but she knew it was coming. Her husband had been making pointed comments about how their son still needed to get to school and how he would be back at work soon. She had tried to avoid his suggestions about shopping and fresh air, but instead she curled up in a small ball looking at the front door, which both terrified and beckoned her. She wasn't used to feeling trapped, being a prisoner in her home and a hostage in her own body.

Her mother had been visiting during one of his pointed conversations, and they'd had a thunderous argument in the living room. Her mother stood, arms akimbo, screaming about how her daughter had had a traumatic life-changing experience and how he was being a complete dick.

The wife had sat quietly through the exchange, silently willing the two people to stop screaming. Yes, her husband was being an ass, but he had a point. Life was going to move on at some point, and the little boy who was now laid on the sofa needed her to be the best mother she could be. She could not let this taint her son's life.

The Owners of the Terrace

The wife of the terrace plumped the cushions on her sofa for the fifth time, the estate agent would be here in ten minutes. They were selling the house. She began to check the living room again and saw something stuffed between the sofa cushions. It was a newspaper. The headline read "RAPE." Her husband must have stuffed it down there; he wasn't coping well. He felt guilty that a crime had happened outside of their home while he slept. He was exhausted and under the doctor's care. Sleeping tablets had been prescribed, but more often than not, she awoke to find him sitting at the window, watching and waiting. Like the large hound her grandfather had kept as security.

He was determined to avoid sleep in case he missed something else. He kept a notebook by the window and kept a written log about the people who walked past, including times, dates, what they wore, and how they acted. He was becoming obsessed with the comings and goings of the forest path. He wore clothes in case he needed to leave quickly, and trainers were laced tightly on his feet in case he needed to run after someone. He was like a loaded gun, poised and ready to fire.

The doctor had said he was suffering from insomnia, anxiety, and depression and had signed him off work for two weeks. She, on the other hand, was coping fine, and it was becoming a source of contention between them. Seeing and hearing about these sorts of events was second nature to her; she'd administered morning-after pills to drunk girls who woke up in strangers beds, pulled glass out of the faces of people who had been violently beaten in bar fights, and comforted women who had been sexually assaulted. That's not to say she wasn't uneasy; this was closer to home. She kept wondering if the people she saw in the supermarket were friends of the woman and if the man carrying flowers was her husband trying desperately to bring some happiness back into his wife's life. The victim's face would be imprinted on her mind forever. And what of the rapist? Was it the man who sold them lottery tickets in the corner shop? The man who changed the tyres on her cars six months ago? Was it a friend of theirs? She was looking at everyone with suspicion.

She had made the decision to sell after yet another sleepless night, finding her husband sitting at the window, and another day of crossing the street to avoid every man she met. They needed a fresh start. A new place to call home, one that was safer, one where they didn't jump every time they heard someone walking down the woodland path.

The estate agent told them they'd take a loss; everyone in the town knew about the incident and where it had happened. People didn't pay high amounts for houses next to crime scenes; women didn't want to hang their families washing ten feet from where another woman had been raped. She didn't care about the money; she wanted her husband back in bed with her, cocooned around each other, protecting themselves against the world in the sanctuary of each other's skin.

The Watcher, the Waiter, the Hunter

The hunter sat in the bath of his new apartment. He was relaxed, the water surrounding him was filled with soap, hair, and scum. He got out and drained the tepid fluid, feeling content. He towelled himself dry and threw on the new bathrobe he had treated himself to. It was Oxford red, the colour of fresh blood, and beautifully soft. It made him feel like he was being enveloped in a warm hug. He sat down on the sofa and thanked his lucky stars that the flat came fully furnished. He had brought hardly anything with him. Ready to make a quick getaway if he needed to. But he shouldn't need to; this was his fresh start.

He had driven here immediately after finishing his mediocre breakfast in the cafe and had been nervously watching the news since trying to work out if he had gotten away with his crime.

The photo fit had only just been released, "artists rendition" had been printed below. He grabbed the newspaper he'd had delivered off the side and looked at the sketch carefully. It looked nothing like him now. The man in the picture had a beard, and due to his recent bath, he was clean-shaven. All evidence of his previous beard was now swirling down the plug hole. Another piece of evidence ready to enter the counties sewers. And the picture didn't really look like him anyway; the nose was far too big for a start.

He was sure there was no way to link him to the rape. This was his current address, far from the town the incident had happened in. It had been for weeks. He had been seen entering the cafe before the incident, and he had no beard. He was safe.

The only thing that linked him to the victim was the pair of her knickers that he had taken from the scene and placed in a safe at the back of his wardrobe. He had chosen the date of the attack as the combination; sure no one would ever crack it. It also gave him a thrill of pleasure to know what he was hiding, to know that he had gotten away with his crime, and to know that he could revisit the memory by simply typing in six digits.

He was safe and happy, free of the pain and guilt that the people of the victim's town and her family were facing. He was starting a new job tomorrow in a new factory. Nobody here knew who he was or what he had done. He was starting a new life. He could reinvent himself. He could be anyone he wanted to be. He could be the joker, the friendly neighbour, the concerned colleague, or the romancer. But this time he would be sensible; he wouldn't let a temptress's call put him in such danger again. He would be good.

The Husband

The husband had been back at work for a week now. Luckily, his return had coincided with the school holidays, so his wife had been left with plenty of time to prepare for her return to normal life. She seemed to be coping much better; she had stopped wearing her scruffy dressing gown and was now dressing in jeans and long hoodies. Ill-fitting shapeless clothes that made her look more like a man than a woman. The husband was sure this was her intention after the incident, but he found it off-putting.

His mother-in-law had continued her interference by telling some of his wife's friends what had happened. Sharing the embarrassment of the news with other people, telling them the gritty details, and parading the difficulty of their situation in front of strangers. The last week of his leave had been spent making cups of green tea for the various hippies and artists who had entered his home.

A gay couple his wife was friends with had brought a huge bouquet of flowers that they'd grown themselves, which now filled the house with vivid scents and left stains on the furniture and carpets.

Simone, an exuberant actress, had come down from London for the day. Brandishing the energy of a woman on a mission, she had carefully washed the blood from his wife's hair and cut it into a sleek style that she exclaimed was "Audrey Hepburn-esque". The husband didn't like it though. He thought the closely cropped hair made his womanly shaped wife look like a little boy, especially when paired with the boxy clothes she was wearing.

A dreaming yoga instructor had turned up and spent the morning doing complicated poses in the front room with his wife and son, telling her to breathe in positivity and exhale negativity while he stood in the doorway, eyebrows raised. He had been upset to see his son taking part and had tried to lure him away with video games, but it hadn't worked, and the whole time his mother-in-law had sat smugly in the corner drinking yet another cup of decaf tea, knowing that her interference was healing her daughter, whilst his father-in-law was positioned quietly next to her, saying nothing, just watching. His father-in-law was always watching now. He sat by the window, looking at the people passing by, his eyes flickering to the side every time the husband's phone so much as vibrated. He could constantly feel his father in law's silent judgement.

The last person to arrive was his wife's ex-boyfriend. He had found out from one of the other friends and immediately turned up on the doorstep, looking more dishevelled than the husband remembered. He hated that the ex and his wife had remained friends. The ex claimed he was living in a small town on the coast, working on fishing boats by day and on his "art" at night, but apparently, he had dropped everything to come and support his "darling muse". What a prick, the husband had thought to himself.

The husband had seen pictures of this man's art. One such piece was currently residing in his loft, hidden behind the shroud of a black bin liner. He had wrapped it up in the pretence of keeping it safe until he found the right place to hang it, creating stories about wall plugs and special screws. But really, it was because he hated to look at it. Realistically, he'd like to take a knife to the canvas, carve through the fabric backing, and ruin it once and for all.

The piece featured his wife reclining on a bed, reading a book, naked, and painted in lurid colours. The ex had boasted how the husband's wife had taught him to appreciate the female form and how his wife's love of colour had inspired his "exhibition" and his life. The husband hated that man, yet another man who had seen his wife's naked body and touched her intimately. Was there any male on the planet that she wouldn't let fuck her? Was it even rape, or had she just drawn attention to herself in her typical way? Maybe she had led this man on with her promises and smiles; maybe she had been caught and found herself spinning a lie. Maybe he himself had been caught by her and her blatant sexuality. He could have done far better than her, so why was he still here?

The ex's biggest crime were the gifts he brought. His present to his "darling," as he liked to call her, was stacks of canvas, tubes of paint, and hundreds of brushes. Great tufted ones, soft as kitten fur, tiny detail brushes made up of only one or two hairs. He brought pastels, paper, and charcoal he had made himself from burning beach driftwood. His son had been in awe of this wild man who stepped into their tidy dining room like he owned it and exclaimed that it would be the perfect place for a studio.

He had taken the table cloth from the table, thrown it on the floor, sat his wife there, and then gently placed a paintbrush in her hand. Claiming "art heals".

But the husband had seen the fear in her eyes, as she hadn't painted in years. He knew she wouldn't remember how, but this hadn't perturbed her ex. Instead, he had plonked their son on her knee and made them paint together. They splotched paint on the canvas messily. Making shapes and letting the paint run down onto the table the husband had chosen so carefully for its quality and solid wood design. The stains they left would never come out. The result was a mess of colour, with hearts and lines and sloppy brush marks going over the edges.

After they had finished, the husband had seen the ex whispering to his wife about how "it would come," and he had watched them embrace. He tried to remember the last time he and his wife had even touched. Not since after the incident, but had they before? The husband didn't really enjoy the feeling of physical contact, preferring instead to keep those he lived with at arm's length.

Later, after the ex had finally gone, proclaiming that he wasn't far away and a trip to the sea might do his old girlfriend good, the husband had come back into the house to find his father-in-law hammering nails into his pristine magnolia walls under the instruction of his young son so they could hang his newly painted picture. He had given his beaming son a strained smile while dust drifted onto his pristine floors and the still wet paint left marks across the wall. Larger wet patches had dripped directly onto the carpet, leaving a trail of dark red clots that looked unnervingly like blood. At that point, he realised he couldn't wait to get back to work. He couldn't wait to get back to normal. To escape the hell his wife had created for him.

So far, work was going smoothly. A whole office full of people seemed to know what had happened, and they were being a lot nicer to him. His welcome-back interview hadn't gone so well. His manager had sat sternly at his desk, telling him that his behaviour with his secretary had been unacceptable and that under normal circumstances he would have been fired. However, due to the current circumstances, he was willing to let it slide, provided it never happened on company property or time ever again.

The husband had breathed a sigh of relief. His job was safe, and so was his mistress. They would be free to continue their entanglement as long as no one else found out and he was careful. He would keep his mistress on a leash and be a good husband to his wife. Everything would be back to normal soon. He could keep his life in perfect balance.

The Son

Mummy was broken. There was no other way to put it. She wasn't smiling anymore, and her clothes were wrong. The son couldn't pick her out in a crowd anymore, not in the jeans and jumpers she was wearing. She looked like all the other mums. He knew she still had her pretty dresses. He'd seen them hanging in the wardrobe.

She looked poorly too; her skin had been covered in a pattern of big purple blotches and angry red marks, but it looked better now. Her face still looked tired though. He wanted to know what had happened, but Daddy had told him not to ask Mummy what was wrong, so he didn't.

At least Daddy was back at work now; him being home had been awful. He tutted when Mummy dropped things, which she did a lot now, and he shouted at her when she cried about going to the shop. Mummy never normally cried about shopping; at least she hadn't before.

Today he had heard the ice cream van in the street, and he had dragged Mummy out of the house for a lolly. It had been hard work; her feet seemed to get stuck with every step she took, like she was wading through thick mud, and she had hesitated when they got to the van. She wouldn't look the man serving them in the eye and had practically run back to the house after he got his rocket ship lolly.

Afterwards, she went upstairs for a long time and cried. The son had felt very guilty about asking for an ice lolly. He felt a dark pit of uncomfortable tension in his tummy and tried desperately to think about what he might have done to make Mummy cry.

The ~~Dog~~ Owner

The ex-dog owner was sitting and staring at the sleeping tablets in his hand. He had been hoarding his prescription. He couldn't cope anymore. Getting up and going to work every day, trying to live his life for just himself. It wasn't working; he didn't feel his life was enough of a reason to live.

He looked at the note he had left on the table for his sister, making sure that he had told her how much he loved her and checking it for spelling errors. He had also left a brief note at the bottom asking her to apologise to his boss. It seemed rude to kill yourself and leave your boss in the lurch, but it wasn't as though he could let him know in advance.

Everything was in order. He started scrolling through pictures of his beloved dog on his phone and got ready to take his first tablet when he heard a scratching at the window. He tried to ignore it, but suddenly a loud meowing came as well.

He looked out of the window and saw a small kitten perched on his window ledge. How could something so small make so much noise? "Fuck," he muttered to himself. A storm was raging outside, and he couldn't leave the kitten outside to get drenched; that would be cruel. He opened the window and grabbed the kitten by the scruff of the neck. "Well, what are you doing here?" The cat meowed again. It was tiny, fitting neatly into the palm of his hand. The dog owner hated cats; they were aloof and belonged to no one. They didn't have the loyalty of dogs.

The Incident

He placed the kitten on the floor and walked into his kitchen in search of milk. He found none in the fridge. He sighed and looked at the kitten that had followed him, still meowing. Really, he thought to himself. Another animal had come at his time of need. What was he, Noah?

He carefully let himself out of his home, telling the kitten that he would be back soon, and drove to the nearest pet shop for kitten supplies. When he returned home, the kitten was curled up in his treasured dog's bed. He set up the flat first, putting kitten food into one of his cherished dog Bella's old bowls and lining a new litter tray with newspaper, the police sketch of an unknown rapist looking up at him. Ready to be shat on.

He sat up through the night, checking that the kitten was still breathing and occasionally feeding it milk from the end of his finger. He had to laugh; once again, he had been saved from the point of no return by an animal. He threw the pills down the sink, ripped up the letter, threw it in the bin, and decided that Bella was as good a name for a cat as it had been for a dog.

The Wife, the Mother, the Woman, the Victim

The mother sat on the bottom step of the stairs and tied her shoelaces. It was the first day of the new term, and she was ready. She'd been trying really hard recently. She'd made plans with friends, tried hard to please her husband, and left the house on her own three times without panicking. The only thing she hadn't succeeded in was painting. A stack of canvas lay unadorned in the corner, mocking her with their white empty spaces. They were a mirror of herself.

Her son was waiting by the door, a school backpack square on his small shoulders. It contained a lunch she had made, in her kitchen, using food she had brought from the supermarket by herself. She was providing. She was coping. Or at least she was trying too.

She took three deep breaths, opened the door, and began to walk, holding tightly to her son's petite hand. Using her small child as an anchor, the mother started her first steps back into normality.

~~The Old Man~~

The old man was not drinking his regular cup of tea in his kitchen, nor was he smoking a secret cigarette down at the bottom of the garden. He was gone.

Instead, his son sat at the kitchen table of the small house, trying to come to terms with what had happened. His father had hung up on him; he had ripped the phone out of the wall, and then he had sat in the living room and quietly had a heart attack.

The son hadn't known that his father had died when he lay in bed with his girlfriend. He hadn't realised when his father didn't answer the phone for their weekly phone call. It was only after his father's doctor had called him about a missed appointment that he even considered something might be wrong with the man who had given him life.

He had driven down immediately, banging on his father's door and upturning all the flower pots, trying to find the one that hid the spare key. Poppies and gardenias were strewn across the path like a blanket. When he finally entered the house, he found his father lying on the floor in front of his favourite chair. A picture of his mother as a young woman was on the table above the body. It had been his father's favourite picture, the one he always found a frame for, the one he had carried in his breast pocket close to his heart when he walked into war to do his duty.

The son had phoned an ambulance and cradled his father's head on the floor. Two men who never understood each other lying on the floor, and the woman who had united them smiling above.

The Husband

The husband sat rigidly at his desk, desperately trying to explain his situation to his secretary yet again. She was angry, and rightly so. Since the incident her life had changed. She no longer visited hotel rooms with her lover, and the manager was being downright cold towards her. Treating her like a common whore.

The rumour mill had been working overtime, and now the whole office knew about the affair. The women whispered behind their hands about how men were cheating bastards and scowled at him. One male colleague had even questioned why he would "bang" his secretary when he had such a beautiful, vibrant wife at home.

Everyone knew his wife; she was considered a delight at the Christmas party, dancing with everybody from the office, comforting drunken accountants in toilets at the end of the night, and announcing the charity tombola. His colleagues had been horrified to hear what had happened to her. He looked like an asshole, and he hated the way people were thinking of him now.

He considered his situation; he had funds to spare. He would ask his mistress to quietly leave her job and set her up in a flat of her own until they could be together. He would be in control once again.

Little did he know that the mistress had plans of her own. She was fed up with sneaking around and lying; she wanted what she considered hers by right. She had planted evidence everywhere she could think, nude pictures in his briefcase, graphic and sexy love notes in the pocket of his coat, and a pair of her most scandalous panties hidden under the front seat of his car. Now all she had to do was wait.

The Son

They didn't walk to school the same way now, taking the main road instead of the woodland path. It was longer and less pretty, but at least it was still just him and Mummy. She was still singing and smiling, but for the first time in the son's short life, he noticed the smile wasn't quite reaching his mother's eyes.

The Wife, the Woman, the Mother, the Victim

The woman had dropped her son off at school, the teacher had come out and hugged her tightly, whispering in her ear that if she needed anything, just let her know. It had been awkward and uncomfortable to think that people had this personal knowledge of her now. And worse, to think that they thought they could do anything to fix it. Like they had that power.

She was looking forward to chatting with the old man and trying to forget the events of the previous weeks. However, instead of a friendly wave and greeting, she found his house being emptied by a stranger. She called out and asked where the man was. He had died.

The woman sucked in air, shocked. Trying to fill her lungs to stop herself from crying, tears came so easily now. Her eyes contained great oceans that were ready to spill at any moment. She wished she had known the old man better; she wished she had taken the time to learn more about his life and to invite him around for a cup of tea. Instead, he had died alone, surrounded by the relics of his past.

The strange man asked if she knew his father, and she told him not really, only in passing. She motioned to the upturned flower pots and commented on how lovely she had found his garden. The strange man told her to wait and went back into the house. Her palms started sweating, and she wondered if she should leave. If she should turn on her heel like a child and run. She hoped he wouldn't invite her in. She couldn't cope with being in a cold and empty house with a strange man she didn't know.

Luckily the strange man walked out with a Pyrex dish in his hands, it had been hastily filled with flowers. Poppies, her favourites, were spilling over the edges of the milky white casserole dish, the deep red of the petals a violent contrast. "Take them," he had said "something to remember my father by."

As she walked, she lost herself in thought, remembering the old man. And without knowing, as if on autopilot, she stumbled onto the woodland path once again.

She stood in the place where she had been attacked. The place where a strange man had placed his hands on her body and violated her most private areas. She kicked the dirt and started clawing at the ground as if digging it up would make the pain go away. As if she could bury the memories.

That vile man had destroyed her life. She couldn't bear to let her husband touch her; she was an enigma to her son, she couldn't even wear the clothes she loved for fear that they gave the wrong impression. She had to deal with the sympathetic stares of her friends, with her private business being slapped across the tabloids and debated on the six o'clock news. She was completely broken.

She sat on the earth, crying and waiting. She was waiting for hope, for clarity, waiting for the man who had hurt her to come back and explain his actions. Nothing came, no clarity, no hope, just the realisation that this was what life was now and a choice. She could give up and wither away, let her life die around her, or she could take back what was hers.

The woman stood up, leaving the bowl of Pyrex flowers on the dirt like a gravestone, a monument to her life before the incident. She wasn't fixed, but she was sick of being broken. She walked home, relishing the fresh breeze on her skin, entered her house, picked up one of the paintbrushes her ex-lover had left, and frantically began to paint.

After the Incident – Part Two

They say time heals all wounds. But some scars run too deep to ever fully disappear. Some events cause huge changes in our lives, like moving house, leaving a lover, and having a child. Monumental events that upset the complicated balance of things. We cope with these changes for better or worse because we have no choice.

The Son

The son was a man now. Fifteen years had passed since that dreadful year in which his life had changed. In which his mother had changed. He no longer went to sleep in his childhood bed, dozing as his mother read him stories of elves and wizards while she stroked his head. Now he went to sleep in the arms of his lover, a tall, black-skinned man who made him feel as though his soul was on fire.

His mother had explained what had happened to her as he got older; horrifying conversations, spoken at the paint-stained dining table, where they had both cried and cursed men. As he looked at the beautiful man in his bed, he tried to understand the irony of his situation. His mother had been so badly hurt by a man to the point that it destroyed her life, and here he was starting his life with a being of the same sex.

He hadn't come out to his mother. Instead, he had quite simply introduced her to his current boyfriend one evening. She had been furious.

He hadn't given her a warning; he had just brought this man into her house. She hadn't cleaned, the kitchen was a mess, and the living room was strewn with debris. She was covered in paint. How dare he introduce them like this? She would have baked a cake. She would have at least washed her hands and removed the paint-covered clothing she was wearing. He had to laugh at the contrast between his mother's and fathers' reaction. His father had become tight-lipped and uncomfortable. It was clear that having a gay son was not what his father had expected, and without saying so much as one word against it, he had let all of his feelings be known.

His father's opinion hadn't changed, and he was dreading today. His mother was throwing him a birthday party. Just like she used to when he was young, only with less party hats and more booze. There would still be balloons though, and jelly and pin the tail on the donkey. His mother was a creature of nostalgia, and for her, some things never changed.

And just like every other birthday in his life, his father would be there, judging him and wishing he was different. He kissed his boyfriend to wake him up. They needed to get ready. It was nearly time to leave.

The Husband

The husband stood in front of the house he had once lived in. His pregnant secretary, now his wife, stood by his side, one hand proudly cradling her blossoming belly. The husband hated that belly. They had agreed to have no children, but then suddenly his new wife was talking about biological clocks ticking, and boom, one 'accident' and there it was. A foetus was staring at him through the sonographer's screen, waving and practically laughing at him. The loud heartbeat played over tinny speakers, a marching drum to his new fate.

He ran a hand through his thinning hair, drifted down to his nose, and instinctively stopped to feel the dent. He wondered how on earth he was going to cope with being a parent at his age. He had done his child rearing; now he wanted to relax and enjoy his life. He had enough money, his job was secure, and he had a beautiful wife to come home to every night. A wife who now looked like a bloody whale. He was sure she would get her figure back in no time; after all, she had a very expensive gym membership she could use.

He rang the doorbell and waited patiently whilst his ex-wife fiddled with the countless locks that made her home a fortress. He thought it was overkill. Fifteen years had not dampened her fears, but she was coping well. As much as he hated to admit it.

In fact, she had coped even better after she had thrown him out on the street. Swearing at him for betraying her and chucking a pair of knickers in his face. All he had told her to do was hoover his car, unaware of the surprise his mistress had left under the seat.

At first, he had been angry with the mistress, but she had told him that she'd done it for him to set him free; she loved him, she adored him. Like all narcissistic men, he had lapped up every word and felt pleased with himself for finding a woman he could be proud of, a woman who hadn't been spoiled.

As it turned out, the woman next to him was more of a pain than his first wife. She flirted with colleagues, spent a fortune on expensive clothes while shopping with her girlfriends, and generally did her upmost to make sure she was the absolute centre of attention.

Whilst his first wife had found the limelight organically, his second searched for it like a hungry animal. She made inappropriate jokes, drank far too much, and felt the need for endless displays of affection. Especially in public. And now here she was cradling a belly that was filled with a child he didn't want. A child he was sure she had planned to make sure they had to stay together, a child she was using to one up his previous wife. But he had to soldier on. After all, one failed marriage was unfortunate; two would be a pattern.

~~The Wife~~, The Mother, The Woman, The Victim

The woman stood at her front door, fiddling with the locks and deadbolts that held it shut. She knew it was too many. There were probably banks that had less security than she did but it helped her to feel settled. To help her feel secure.

They had never found the man who hurt her. All the police had were a few drops of unmatched DNA, no sightings, and no suspicious behaviour. Just the woman's word and a medical examination to say she had been raped. Occasionally, on slow news days, local papers would do a feature on the unsolved rape of a young woman during the day. During a weekday morning. They would phone the police station and ask if they had any new leads, and the police would reply that the investigation was still ongoing. They had painted this man as a villainous figure comparable to Jack the Ripper or the Zodiac Killer, faceless but still at large. A local celebrity. The papers had even given him his own moniker, "the beast of the woods". He became a town myth, a fable that was told to wayward young girls who needed the fear of God putting in them. The type of story that meant the older women of the town still didn't feel quite comfortable with popping to the shops for a pint of milk alone.

The victim had phoned the police helpline on the first Monday of every month for an update on her case like clockwork for the past fifteen years. She was sure the police could tell it was her from the day and time she called. She knew all of the officers who answered the phone by name and voice. The police officer she had met at the hospital, now a sort of friend, was still in charge of her case. That police officer was a mother now, and the victim had sent a card and flowers to celebrate the birth of her newborn baby. A boy.

The victim tried not to think of the boy one day growing into a man and hurting some poor woman. But she couldn't help it; she thought it of all the little boys she met. Will you become a rapist? Will you hurt women? Will you force yourself on them as they cry? The thought always ran through her head as she cradled the small babies in her arms. She blushed at the unspoken words whilst admiring friends' babies and tried to ignore the voice in her head telling her that this child could be. She tried to think positively; there's not a chance in hell any of her friends would raise a rapist. As a mother, she would hate to have someone think her son could be capable of that. But then maybe her attacker's mother thought he was innocent. That mother couldn't have known as she rocked her son's crib that one day, he would plunge so deep into a woman that he would break her very soul. Maybe he was the kind of man to bring his mother flowers for no reason. Who mowed her grass and washed her pots when he visited. Maybe he had girlfriends who would have attested to his good nature and gentleness.

And what of the rapist's father? Had he looked into his son's eyes and seen darkness? Had he thought his son might be capable of horrific acts as he taught him to ride his bike and tie his shoelaces?

The Incident

She had come to terms with the situation now. She ignored the nagging voice that said the man was still out there somewhere in the world. At large, as they had said in the paper. She tried not to wonder if he had hurt anyone else. There had been no DNA matches in the past fifteen years, so she assumed not, but maybe he had just been more careful. Maybe he had chosen not to stain another woman's clothing. Maybe he had done it slyly; date rape was all the rage, small blue pills slipped into drinks, making women feel woozy. Tiny blue pills that undressed women and opened legs all on their own.

But the woman had moved on, and so had her life. She had thrown her cheating husband out. Yes, he had stayed a while after the incident, but things had gone from bad to worse. He had less patience with her now, no patience for their home, and he seemed to start exerting more and more of a right over her life and body. He tried to stop her friends from coming over, suggesting it could have been one of them who had hurt her.

It got worse with her body though. Her husband was a sexual man, something she seemed to have forgotten before the attack when he was working long nights and coming home smelling strange. Although he had barely touched her before the incident, he now seemed to have a carnal need to exert his claim on the territory of her body once more. One night he had clearly come to bed feeling as though he deserved sex for looking after her; he was owed sex from his wife, it was his right. He needed gratitude.

But the wife hadn't been ready. She had to fight him off, her own husband, and although she broke and scarred his nose in the process, blood spewing onto their clean sheets, she had already forgiven him in the morning when she loaded them into the washer. She tried to ignore the fact that her last two sexual encounters had ended with bloodshed and had been happy to try and carry on at her own pace until she found the lacy knickers in his car. Then she completely lost her mind.

Everything she had ignored prior to her attack was now staring her right in the face and arrogantly smiling. The long work nights, the endless leaving dos, and the strange smell that followed her husband. She found out that it was his secretary. A woman who had been so kind to her at the Christmas party and who had complimented her on her dress and shoes. This woman had stalked her way around her husband like a predator and marked him with her scent like a common alley cat. And her husband had let her.

As she grew older, she realised it was for the best. The husband wasn't actually that good at being a husband. He was cold and controlling. He wasn't a brilliant father unless outside eyes were on him, then he was all smiles and kisses. Dad of the year.

The woman finally managed to open the door, apologising to the guests that stood in front of her. Her husband, still tall, still tidy but older, and his new wife. She was young and sunny and looked like the sort of woman you see on a reality television program about trying to find true love. An optimistic idiot. But now she was huge. Clearly, she had no trouble offering her body to the man who had once been her own husband, and it showed.

Inwardly, the wife laughed. Her husband must hate this. In the years after their son had been born, she had begged and pleaded for a second child, another person to love with all of her heart, someone for their son to grow up with, a playmate, a confidant, and her husband had always said no. Claiming another baby would add years onto them getting their lives back. Another decade of nappies and nightmares. Now here he was due to become a father in his mid-fifties with a wife who was probably already screwing her personal trainer.

She was over it now; all of the venom she felt towards her husband and his new wife had gone. Now she only looked on them in pity, two bland people, living a bland, colourless life, always in fear of what other people would say. Her life was full of colour again. Always full of surprise, always with an underlying anticipation about what might happen next.

The Watcher, the Waiter, the Hunter, the Husband

The victim's husband wasn't the only one to find a new wife; the hunter had too. It had happened suddenly. He had started his new job, and there on the line was a young woman who was shy and retiring. Her hands were always screwed up into fists, and when she sat, she seemed to take up no space at all, as if she were trying to eclipse her own existence. He spoke to her a few times and realised that she was what his mother would have cruelly called "not the full shilling". But she clung to him, always sitting and eating lunch with him, listening to his every word like he was the new messiah.

The hunter liked it. This was the type of woman he needed. Someone who understood how important he was, someone who could adore him. He asked her on a date his second week in the job, and she accepted, blushing and giggling like a young school girl. He liked her innocence. Well, she was young, twenty years younger than he was.

At first, he thought it was strange that she wouldn't let him drive her to her door after their dates, but then one night he understood why. She had left her cardigan in his car, and as he pulled up outside her house to give it back, he could hear her father screaming at her, calling her a whore. As he entered the house, he saw her father standing above her with his fist raised, and anger flooded through him. The watcher grabbed his girlfriend and pulled her inside his car whilst she cried, and her father continued his barrage of hateful words. He took her back to his flat and proposed. They had been together ever since. He used the one good ring his mother owned as an engagement ring; the one item he had hurriedly taken from her lifeless corpse after the pills drifted had her away to a long overdue death.

They hadn't had a long engagement, just long enough to find two willing witnesses and a venue. Neither of them had any friends, and both of their families were now estranged or dead, so it was a small affair. His wife had worn a pink dress from the local charity shop instead of white, and they had gone for drinks in the local pub after. A few of the other workers from the factory had met them there, holding cheap cards that their wives had written and hastily stuffed with five-pound notes.

It was all very modern. In fact, the only traditional thing his new wife wanted was to save herself until her wedding night. The hunter didn't mind. After all, this wouldn't be the first time he had waited for a woman. But things hadn't gone quite as planned after they were married. He had taken her home and walked her to the bedroom. She had sat on the bed and cried. He had asked her if this was her first time. Excitement was flooding through his veins and down to his groin, he'd never been with a virgin before.

It wasn't. Sat on his bed in her pink wedding gown, his new wife told him how for years her father had beaten and abused her. How he had snuck into his room at night and touched her no matter how hard she cried or how loud she shouted. She spoke about how her mother ignored her sobbing until one day she found her in the bathtub, her wrists slit, and the water red with blood. She talked about how she hated her father. About how her new husband had saved her. How he was a good man, a good husband.

The hunter wasn't surprised; he knew the lust men felt. He understood. He wrapped his wife in a hug and told her they could wait until she was ready. Honeyed words wormed into the young woman's heart, melting her from within, and almost instantly he had his way with her.

Their lives had been pretty perfect until his wife surprised him two months into their marriage with a positive pregnancy test. He had never really considered children. He knew he would have given them to the woman he had known in the bright dresses, but to have children with his wife. Well, now he had no choice, and the hunter welcomed a beautiful baby daughter into the world. Another year passed, and beaming his wife gave him another positive test, this time a boy. Enough was enough; he went with his wife to get her tubes burned and tied.

His children were teenagers now; his daughter was reasonably popular with a small group of friends; and his son was a recluse, labelled as weird by the other children and the school.

And the hunter had been good. He hadn't raped another woman; instead, he found new ways to keep himself in check, to keep himself clean and good, and to help control his urges. In the beginning, he found beautiful, exotic, high-class escorts online. His wife never checked their bank account, so he would book repeat appointments with them until their madams deemed them too busy to be available. The girls were all booked up. They proffered excuses like bouquets of flowers. Apparently, all of the girls he wanted were otherwise occupied.

Then he sought prostitutes on street corners and alleyways, dirty girls who he knew were beneath him. But slowly they became wary of him too; even the lowest heroin whore wouldn't take his money. Even the most disgusting women who had worked the streets for years and had countless men take them roughly against brick walls began to cower from his touch. He saw them group together when he walked towards them, whispering about how he was creepy and strange.

Yes, he had asked them to do things, things that were different from what they were used to. But it was his right; he was paying for a service, and he wanted his money's worth. At first, they didn't mind when he asked them to let him fuck them outside. They looked concerned when he asked them to scream and downright terrified when he asked them to close their eyes and not move. To play dead, or at least unconscious.

But the real problem was the watching. The girls complained to their pimps and madams about an unsettling feeling of being watched after they had been with him. About footsteps heard on the stairs and shadows outside of their windows. Yes, he had followed them, but only because he was curious. He wanted to learn more about them, and they should be grateful for his interest. One went home to her lesbian lover, who was also a prostitute. Another went home to a syringe full of heroin and a dirty mattress, and one even went home to her husband and children, claiming that her shift at the pub had been crazy and insisting that she needed a shower because she smelled of sweat and beer, when in reality she smelt like the ten men she had managed to get through her cunt in one night.

He liked watching them; he felt a better connection when he saw them in their day to day lives, cooking, cleaning, and sleeping. But clearly, they found it unnerving, and over the past months, the deep pool he had enjoyed swimming in had dried up. He was tired and frustrated and would have to look elsewhere for his needs.

The Husband

The husband took a moment to stare at the house he had once lived in. It was a mess. Blankets were strewn across sofas and tables; books were piled up against walls, used as coffee tables, half-empty cups of tea rested on top of them and the surface of every beige wall was covered. Handmade wall hangings from Tibet, canvas' his son had painted, pages torn from sketch books were taped to the walls, and in the middle of the hallway scrawled in sharp angry letters were the words "It is my body, I shall take possession of it". The husband used his forefinger to trace the word "body" and tried to think when his wife could have written it.

After the incident, definitely after he had left. He caught his new wife looking at him with a confused expression on her face, and he quickly pulled his arm away "you should paint over that" he said roughly "it's unsightly".

His ex-wife rolled her eyes. She mocked him openly now. The young woman he had known had risen like a phoenix from the ashes and was stronger than ever. Her hair was still shortly cropped, and she still wore baggy, shapeless clothes, but they were filled with colour again. Flared trousers hung off her, pooling gently at her bare feet; a large flowered men's shirt was tucked in at her waist and layers of necklaces were wrapped around her neck, glinting in the light. She looked effortless. She no longer dressed for the pleasure of him or other men. Instead, she dressed for herself, and he was pretty sure she was braless.

As she bent over to pick up one of the many cats that now seemed to occupy his old home, her shirt had fallen forward, exposing the breasts that used to be his. The ones he used to touch but now couldn't. He tried not to stare. He knew his wife was watching, and he couldn't, for even one second, give her any reason to think their lives were less than perfect.

She walked the husband and new wife outside, not caring to put shoes on her feet; instead, she walked across grass and stones and directed them to some chairs. The husband didn't notice that his new wife's chair was the most comfortable of the assortment. An old rocking chair that his ex had dragged downstairs from their son's room, huffing and puffing so the expectant mother wouldn't be too uncomfortable.

It was a grand gesture. His previous wife had rocked their son in that chair when he was a baby, and here she was offering it to his pregnant new wife. Her replacement. But the husband didn't notice. He only noticed how his own chair had uneven legs and was tilting unsteadily on the patio like a drunk. Plus, he was distracted by the faces of two people he most definitely didn't want to see.

His previous wife's ex-boyfriend had become a permanent fixture in her life after the incident. He had clung to his previous wife, attempting to guide her through the perilous waters of her life, and to make matters worse, his son adored him. Free-spirited people were always adored by children, and this man was no exception. He took him sailing, he played guitar and knew all of the constellations by heart. The husband tried to ignore him at these events, but here he was offering him a beer. A fucking beer. He had lived in this house; he had fucked the host within its walls, he could get his own dammed beer, it was his right. He wondered if the ex-boyfriend was fucking her, and for how long? Would they fuck or would they make love? He remembered basking in his ex-wife's body, and the thought of that scruffy lout doing the same made him feel sick to his stomach. He took his eyes off the ex-boyfriend.

The other person he didn't want to see was his ex mother in law. The old cow was still holding on to each and every molecule of life she had. Old age makes most people more timid, but not her. She was still filled with energy and more obnoxious than ever. Talking loudly and telling the same stories over and over again, like a scratched record stuck on repeat. No doubt they would be hearing her favourites today, how she had been a dancer in her youth, how she had kissed two of the Beatles, and how even at her age she had fended off a mugging by battering the young hooligan with her walking stick. The husband drained his beer in one foul swoop. It was going to be a long day, and his firstborn son wasn't even here yet.

The Son

The son tapped his fingers impatiently on the steering wheel. He was nervous. He was always nervous to see his father. As a child he had idolised him, but now that he was older, he could see the glaring flaws in his character. These flaws had become more pronounced since the son had exposed his sexuality to the world. His father clearly didn't want a homosexual for a child, but here he was gay and proud with a beautiful man by his side, and it was his birthday. Nothing could ruin it.

He pulled onto the driveway of his childhood home and saw balloons attached to the door. His mother, as always had pulled out all the stops. Every year, he tried to get her to tone it down, but she wouldn't. He knew the house would be full of balloons, that his birthday cake would have exactly the right number of candles for his age, and that his mother would light fireworks as soon as it got dark.

He rang the doorbell and waited for his mother to answer the door and unlock her castle. He often wondered how he would get into the house if his mother had an accident, but he had decided long ago that he would barge the door down with his car if he had to, he would smash windows and pull the bricks out one by one with his bare hands. Nothing would separate him from his mother if she needed him.

The door flew open, and his mother surrounded him with a hug. Then she pulled his boyfriend into the embrace as well. She led them through the house. Past his paintings, past postcards he had sent from his holidays, and snapshots of them throughout the years. The house was a glorious scrapbook of their lives. He especially liked their early work together.

They had thrown paint at large canvases after his father left, cleansing their souls. At first, they had been crying, but in the end, after they saw the paint splattered across the canvas and most of their garden, they had laughed. They had hung them on the walls and occasionally added to them. His mother had drawn a charcoal portrait of him on one, and he had written some poetry on another, words scribbled out and underlined. A first draft.

As he entered the garden, his grandma's voice was the first thing he heard, ringing out like a church bell on Sunday. "Where is my Adonis?" His boyfriend pushed his way forward and allowed himself to be held by the old woman. She loved his boyfriend, striking an unlikely friendship based on art and culture. He saw the love in her eyes as she cupped his boyfriend's face with her hands, white leather against smooth ebony. She had called him Adonis since the first moment she had seen him, claiming that men that good-looking were not of this earth. The son had wondered if his grandmother might scare the shy boy he loved so much, but he had laughed, and the two of them had been thick as thieves ever since.

His boyfriend immediately sat at his grandmother's side, filling the space his grandfather had left. His grandfather's death had been a blow to them all. His quiet ways had left bigger silences than any of them could ever have imagined. But they all took comfort in the fact that he had died as he had lived, quietly listening to his wife talk as she knitted yet another blanket to cover his body. As if the grim reaper would get confused with the mounds of woollen squares acting as armour and give up trying to find him. In fact, when an ambulance was finally called and the paramedic asked how long his grandfather had been unresponsive, his grandmother had frankly replied that she had been knitting and he hadn't really responded since their first year of marriage when he asked her to put more salt in the potatoes in the future, so it was hard to tell how long he'd been dead for.

His eyes flicked to the end of the table where his father was sitting, looking extremely uncomfortable. The doorbell rang again, and he saw his father flinch as a hoard of people came in. It was a mixed bunch. His high school girlfriend walked through the door; she had taken the news of his sexuality well, claiming she had no idea but that she wanted him to be happy anyway. Two cars full of university friends, already half drunk and ready to party, were strolling through the house, commenting on the decor and the art that hung on the walls. A few of his mother's friends walked in, people who had become fixtures in their lives after his father had left. Simone, who had slept on their sofa for two months after a director fired her for not sleeping with him, the gay couple who had helped him navigate his new world of romance and were always on the other end of the phone for advice. His mother's ex-boyfriend was already there. He stood in the corner of the garden by the barbeque, brandishing the tongs like the man of the house.

He had to laugh. This house had no man. It was an equal playing field for all who entered it. Even as a teenager, he had wondered how he could get away with saying things to his mother that other teenagers wouldn't dream of. He supposed it was the nature of the relationship they had built together. They were all each other had.

His eyes closed in on his father again. He was out of place and sat in a hurricane of colour while his bored wife tapped on her phone, ordering more useless stuff for the baby in her belly.

His baby brother. God, it felt weird; he had never craved a sibling like other children he knew. He was perfectly happy to have his mother all to himself. A thought dawned on him. Hopefully this baby brother would be the kind of child his father wanted, a straight man's man, who thought boobs were the bees knees and wouldn't throw his life away on a "useless degree."

His father's words about his future still stung. He was studying psychology, determined to help people with their problems in any way he could. He had seen how lives could be ruined by other people's acts, and he wanted to help other people find their way out of the darkness like his mother had, and more importantly, he wanted to give people the tools so they wouldn't succumb to the darkness in their own souls.

F.Z.CARSON

The Watcher, the Waiter, the Hunter, the Husband

The hunter sat on the carpet of his bedroom with his back firmly against the door. He was taking five minutes of peace away from his life. They had been called into school today because of his son's falling grades. He and his wife had sat on the uncomfortable plastic chairs, listening to the teacher go on about the lack of respect and the attitude his son had been giving out. Apparently there had been arguments in the class-room, something about one of the girls. His wife had been mortified chewing on her finger nails and apolo-gising, like she was the naughty school child. She had left sweat stains on the plastic chairs while she prom-ised they would do better.

The husband was fed up. Life yet again was reaching that boring point he hated, and here he was sitting on the floor, staring intently at a pair of knickers he had taken from the scene of a crime he had committed long ago. He heard a shout from downstairs. His dinner was ready. He returned the underwear to where they were hidden, taking his time to run his finger along the silk and lace and savour their texture. Then he walked into the dining room, ready to eat with his family.

He was surprised as he took his seat at the head of the table, not by the sullen son who sat to his left nor by his teenage daughter, who was chatting animatedly to his right. No, he was surprised by the young girl who was seated next to his daughter, her hair thrown over one shoulder and her fork hovering in the air as she waited to hear the punch line of a joke.

This must be the new friend his daughter had been talking about, the one who had moved to the area after the separation of her parents. She was the one who had openly cried on her first day at a new school and whom his daughter had comforted.

He felt the hunger stir inside him as he watched the young girl slurp spaghetti, tomato sauce hiding in the corners of her smile. He tried to control himself and join the conversation. But as he spoke, he could feel the young girl concentrating on his words, trying desperately to make a good impression on the parents of the only friend she had.

He felt himself becoming aroused and excused himself from the table. As he locked himself in the bathroom, he let all of his old feelings rain down on him. How much he loved women, how he wanted to watch them, to learn their ways, and how, when the time was right, he would take them. He knew it was wrong. If anything, this was worse than the incident with the young woman who had once been the object of his infatuation. This girl was a lot younger; he would have to be more careful.

He began to massage himself through his trousers, anticipation building like it had that day on the woodland path. Slowly but surely, he began to formulate a plan.

F.Z.CARSON

The Young Girl

The young girl hadn't noticed she was staring at her friend's father. Instead, she was actively trying to avoid looking at her friend's brother. He gave off a creepy vibe, and she had already heard rumours about him at her new school. About how he would eat anything for a dare, about how he sat alone at lunch time, the other students were afraid to be associated with him.

But mainly, she was trying to be a good guest. Making friends had been harder than she had thought, especially after she had embarrassed herself by crying on her first day. The girl at her side was her only friend, and she considered being invited around for tea a huge honour. She couldn't screw it up.

Plus, her mother had already warned her to be nice: "You never know when we might need a favour". Her mother had become very keen on favours since the separation. Life as a single parent was hard. She had already convinced their landlord to mow the garden once a week for them because she was too busy. Mrs. Milton, the old woman from next door, had been tasked with making sure the young girl returned from school on the days her mother had work, and another mother from down the road, who had a daughter the year below, somehow found herself offering to drive the young girl to school in the morning.

After all, she was already going that way; why shouldn't the girls share a ride? This favour resulted in the most awkward thirty minutes of the girl's day, sitting in a car with strangers. She dreaded the day the other girl was off sick, and she had to find alternative transport to school.

Her mother was the master of favours and manipulation. But she had to be working two jobs; one as a carer and one as a barmaid, which meant she was hardly ever home, and when she was, she was exhausted. The young girl didn't mind the solitude of her new home. In fact, she quite liked it, and she didn't miss her father at all. His drinking had changed him from the man she loved as a child to a monster, and as far as she was concerned, she wanted nothing more to do with him, no matter how sober he claimed he was.

The Man in the Suit

The man in the suit's life had changed since the incident fifteen years earlier. He no longer had one-night stands with random women. Instead, he had been seeing the same woman for two years and was considering asking her to marry him. He still worked the same job and took the same woodland path every day, but at night he ran.

His running was the reason that a journalist sat in front of him today. He was going to be featured in the local newspaper. "Running for women". A working title.

Since his first run, he had carried on, making his distances further and his runs longer. His calves had thickened, and slowly the blisters on his feet had turned to hard skin. He brought shorts instead of wearing saggy tracksuit bottoms and invested in a decent pair of trainers. Six months after he had found the woman on the path, he ran his first race for a charity specialising in the victims of rape. He became a runner.

After that he hadn't stopped. He ran five kilometres, ten kilometres, half marathons, and this year, for the first time, the London Marathon, all for his favoured charity. He had been asked to run for other causes over the years, but this was his cause, and recently the charity discovered that in just fifteen years he had run over two hundred and fifty races for them, raising over one hundred thousand pounds.

He hadn't realised it, never really noticing the money, just handing it over in a plain envelope. He kept their letters of thanks in a drawer at the bottom of his desk at work and gave his medals to his coworker's daughter to play with. Hope was much older now, but she still had his medals, proudly getting them out and telling people about her token uncle and his charity work.

The charity had offered to name their new building after him. To have his name above the door of a sanctuary for women felt wrong, so he declined and went back to keeping his head down and doing what he did best. Running. Then one savvy social media guru of the charity office released his stats, including how many races he'd run, for how long, and how much money he had raised. The idea had been to try and boost his Just Giving page for the London Marathon, but the local paper had picked up the story, and he couldn't resist the opportunity to expand his donation net. He said he would do an interview, but only if they made a sizable contribution to his London Marathon donation page and if they provided information on how their readers could donate too.

But now he knew it was a mistake. The woman they had sent was clearly not a journalist looking for a page filling piece. She was asking lots of quick-fire questions, and she wanted details. What was the furthest he had run? How often did he train? Did he like running? Why did he always run for this one charity? Did he know someone who was raped? Was he raped?

The man tried to field the questions as best he could. He gave his stats and figures, kindly printed off for him by someone in the charity office, and tried to avoid the rape question. But the journalist wouldn't give up. She wasn't stupid. She knew people only ran that many races for one cause if they had a deep and meaningful connection with it.

She asked the question again, "do you know someone who was raped?" Her pen was poised in the air as he stumbled over his reply; he didn't, well, not properly. He told the short version of the story, about how he had helped someone after they had been raped and how he had been determined to try and help more women.

The journalist had tried asking more questions about the woman, but he brushed them off, not wanting to get into the gritty details of the day that still haunted him. Then the journalist took him outside to take some photographs to accompany the story. In her emails she had suggested he stood tall, hands on hips, while a group of women gazed adoringly up at him from his feet, but he had squashed it immediately. Then she suggested that he wear all of his medals; they could loop them over his arms if they needed to. He replied that he didn't actually have any of his medals. The journalist looked at him exasperated and settled instead for a fairly nice picture of him in his running gear, crouched down, tying his shoelace.

It was published on the third page of the local newspaper, underneath an article about a failing local school.

~~The Wife~~, the Mother, the Woman, the Victim

Debris from the party was strewn around the house, streamers still hung from the ceiling, a small pile of cigarettes were stubbed into a half-eaten slice of cake, and her mother was asleep on the sofa. Half an empty bottle of wine at her side. She always ended up on the sofa after parties. A bed was made for her upstairs, but fear of missing out meant she never used it, preferring instead to collapse wherever she landed, normally halfway through one anecdote or another.

The party had been good; her ex-husband had left fairly early after his new wife had made a few pointed comments about how tired she was, gesturing to her expanding stomach and staring the woman directly in the eye, challenging her to say something about the baby she was carrying.

Her son had opened his presents, and the wrapping paper was still floating around the table. She had painted him a picture of his boyfriend; his grandmother had given him his grandfather's gold watch, scuffed but still full of memories and his father had given him a gift card for a popular men's clothing shop. Now he and his lover were sleeping on a blow-up mattress in her studio at the end of the garden.

They called it her studio, but really it was a ramshackle collection of sheds her father had cobbled together after her first art exhibition had gone well and she had been commissioned for another. She had been in a rut, struggling with what her next collection should be based on, when her father said she needed more space and had come home with a borrowed van bearing various bits of sheds he had acquired from friends.

She still remembered the day they erected it in the garden. Her small son had stood seriously with a hammer, carefully bludgeoning nails wherever his grandfather instructed him. Tongue sticking out with concentration, his hair sticking to his forehead with the sweat of the summer heat. Together, they had painted the interior white, and her mother had arrived with various rugs thrifted from charity shops and friends. They covered the hard wooden floor and the jutting out nails her son hadn't quite hammered home. It was her haven.

She had created all of her best works in that studio, landscapes of dark moors her ex took her to, where they talked and held hands in the moonlight. Commissioned works from families who wanted traditional portraits to hang above their fireplaces, a status symbol for those who had really made it in the world, and when times were hard and money was tight, she made small sketches of people's loved ones and pets for ten pounds each.

Her ex had rekindled her love of art, pulling it out of her piece by piece like he had so many other aspects of her nature. He had been the first man she had sex with after the incident. A cold night two years later, where she explained to him her yearning for another human's flesh and her fear. He had held her as she explained her violation and justified her need for the love of another. They had agreed they would try; they were friends, closer than she and her husband had ever been. Two souls gently entwined enough to stay close to one another but not tight enough to hold themselves down for fear of hurting each other's feelings.

He had truly surprised her that night. After their agreement, he had come out brandishing paint. He instructed her to paint the areas she didn't want to be touched in orange. The ones she needed him to be gentle with and take his time in yellow. The ones she thought she would be okay with in green, and the ones she definitely didn't mind in blue. Standing and looking in the mirror of her bedroom, the woman had painted a sexual map on her skin. Covering her mental and physical scars like an abstract portrait.

Afterwards, when they had finished, the sweat and paint had mingled and dripped onto the bed sheet, staining them in a vibrant rainbow of colour, and the woman was relieved to finally have a sexual encounter that didn't end up red.

The Watcher, the Waiter, the Hunter, the Husband

The watcher was making his plan slowly but surely. He had to be careful, as his life was much more complicated now. He couldn't rid himself of the obstacles of his wife and children like he had his mother and the dog.

He knew this would have to be a one-off, perfectly planned. He was excited; after so many mundane years it was nice to have something to focus on. He understood now that he could never have been the man his mother wanted him to be, and he was okay with that. He didn't need anybody else's gratification when he had his own.

He walked into the local pub, a shady establishment with a bad reputation, and found the man he was looking for at the end of the bar. He paid for what he needed and went home to formulate some new lies.

As he got home, he was greeted by a tearful wife. She threw the young woman's underwear in his face, crying and accusing him of an affair. He had so many questions. How did she find them? How had she cracked the code to his safe? His wife replied honestly; she had watched him. She knew he had secrets, and after fifteen years of marriage, she noticed that on a certain date every year, he seemed to be in a world of his own. Withdrawn and unspeaking.

The watcher had been watched.

The Incident

He stood with the lace and silk knickers in his hand and started to lie to his wife. They were his; he lied fluently, the words dripping off his tongue like droplets of water. On the odd occasion he liked to dress up in women's underwear, it wouldn't happen again. She stood staring at him in disbelief, unable to swallow the words he had spoken. It wasn't a full lie. He had once or twice, as a teenager, paraded around in his mother's clothes while she was at work. Wondering what it would be like to be a woman. The fine cotton of his mother's dresses and the silk of her stockings were a sharp contrast to the heavy workwear his father wore.

It was at that moment that he discovered women's weakness. Men's clothes were like armour, hard and sturdy. Practical for the jobs they took and the work they did. Women's clothes were delicate and prone to breaking. Zips split on dresses, and stockings ran with ladders as soon as they were worn. Women were unprotected by their clothes.

He looked his wife in the eyes and begged her to forgive him. She nodded and turned her back on him, ready to forget and continue with the pattern of their lives. She was tired; she had no family and no friends. Without him she had nothing. She too, was trapped.

F.Z.CARSON

The Husband

The party had been painful. He was treated like a stranger by the people around him. Uncomfortable in the place he had once called home. His wife and son were at the centre of the entertainment, talking about things he would never understand, art and feelings. His son's boyfriend had tried to start a conversation with him, but it had been awkward. The young man was studying contemporary dance, a degree more useless, in the father's opinion, than the one his son had chosen. Slowly, the husband's replies had become shorter and less responsive, until finally the boy had just stopped talking. After a few moments, his ex-mother-in-law had called him back, and he had looked relieved to be saved.

His mother-in-law had barely spoken to him, only asking politely how his work was going and how long until the baby was due. She had asked about the baby in a mocking tone; she knew he didn't want more children. She and her daughter had no secrets. She'd have known of his previous wife's constant, irritating begging for another child.

His wife hadn't spoken to anyone. She had spent the time tapping on her phone and yawning in a pointed way. They had a prior agreement that they would leave after cake and presents, but it had been a waste of time. His son had politely thanked him for the gift card but had tears brimming in his eyes when he opened the presents from his mother and grandmother. The husband felt snubbed.

He wondered if he should try to get to know him again. They had lost a lot of their familiarity when he moved out, and there had been some misunderstandings. Such as the curry he had fed him as a child laced with nuts, forgetting his son was allergic, or the holiday he and his wife went on without him when they found out he had chicken pox. They had not wanted to postpone. The holiday was expensive, and they were looking forward to plastering the pictures all over their social media. A perfect family. A perfect couple.

His son had been upset, and instead of spending two weeks in Florida, he had spent two weeks by the sea with his mother in the crumbling cottage that her ex owned. Afterwards, he had seen their own pictures. Candid shots of his still scabby son holding a crab in his hand, wonder etched across his small face, cheeks rosy in delight, and one of his wife walking down the beach barefoot, her head turned slightly over her shoulder as if checking she wasn't being followed or that she wasn't alone.

They said far more than any of the photographs they had taken when they were still a family. Posed, stiff shots taken by a kind passing stranger, only smiling when prompted and with some sort of colossal monument in the background. Later, those shots had been neatly printed and framed by professionals and hung in straight lines on the walls of their once tidy home.

~~The Wife~~, the Mother, the Woman, the Victim

The weekend newspaper thudded on the doormat, a relic from the days when her husband had lived here. He had sat at the kitchen table with a cup of coffee in one hand and a newspaper spread before him. He would read it cover to cover and comment on the articles; he had an opinion about everything.

She had never cancelled the subscription and had only really remembered it when their local shopkeeper informed her that payment for delivery was now going to be done online. Previously, she would have stood with the paper boy, embarrassed, as she dug through purses and jacket pockets, trying to find the correct change. The paper boy stood impatiently on the doorstep, huffing and puffing, checking his watch, but he never seemed to have any change himself.

She cut herself a piece of birthday cake for breakfast and took the newspaper to the garden. She never read it properly. She skimmed the articles that looked interesting and left the boring ones about potholes. Occasionally she would rip out something that inspired her, and that too would end up being taped to the wall with the rest of her scrapbook. But this time, a few pages in, she was greeted with a familiar face.

The man who had saved her. The one who had come to her rescue on that horrible day. The man in the suit. Here he was in technicolour glory, a mixture of tiny dots making up the tones of his skin and the shadows of his face as he crouched down to tie his shoe lace.

He had aged, but she recognised him instantly, and hungrily she began to read the article. He ran; he raised money for a charity that helped victims of rape, people like her. She read it again and ripped it from the newspaper. He hadn't mentioned her directly, but she knew she was the reason he ran; what happened to her was the reason he ran, what had happened to him that day was the reason he ran. He had spoken to the interviewer about how his life had changed, about how he was settled, happy, and glad to help people in this small way.

She took the article into the studio and taped it to one of the walls. Her son and his lover were still asleep on the floor, in a coma of red wine and cake, their bodies entangled together. She grabbed a canvas from a stack nearby and started painting. She had never had a chance to thank him; she had never even seen him again, she had avoided the path he frequented. But now she knew what he had done with his life, she finally knew his name.

She made bold strokes with her brushes, lost in her own world. Painting the face of a man she knew so well, but so little.

The Son

The son awoke to see his partner with his finger to his lips. Beautiful lips that sang sad songs, told no lies, and were perfect for kissing. He motioned to the end of the studio; his mother was there, drawing thick lines onto canvas with a paintbrush, completely lost in her own world. Together, they crept quietly out of the studio, not wanting to disturb her when she was in the moment.

They went into the house and began to tidy up the evidence of the party. Together, they carried the rocking chair back up to his childhood room and placed it on the floor. His boyfriend sat in it and started rhythmically swaying. Suddenly, the son had a vision of his future. His lover sat with a baby in his arms, rocking in the chair the same way his mother had done with him. Two fathers to love it instead of one who just tried. As his mother painted in the garden and his grandmother slept on the sofa, the son realised that this was the perfect place to be in his life. He was happy.

He considered the events that had led to this moment. The betrayal that had led to his and his mother's independence, the honesty with himself that had resulted in the man sitting before him, and the attack that had led to his mother's rebirth.

The Man in the Suit

The man in the suit was surprised by a loud knocking at the door; a cursory glance out of the window had shown a delivery van. He hadn't ordered anything. What on earth was it? A huge box was unloaded as he questioned the grumpy delivery driver. "Sign here" was his answer.

He took the box into the house and began the complicated process of unwrapping all the layers. When he finally got through, he was greeted with a painted image of his own face. It wasn't a posed shot; it was drawn from an odd perspective, as if he were hovering above the canvas. His face looked kind, and his head was surrounded by a dense covering of white paint flecked with yellow. It looked like he had a halo, like sunlight was surrounding him and radiating out of him. He saw the detail in which his eyes had been painted, the faint shadow of a woman in his pupils, and he placed the canvas upright against the wall.

As he did, an envelope fell out from behind it, landing on the floor with a soft thud. Inside was a wad of cash and a handwritten letter.

"I hope you accept this gift; it's how I always remember you.......thank you for what you did. P.s please put the money towards your next run." Instantly, he knew who it was from.

The man in the suit stood speechless, staring at his own beautifully rendered face. He looked like an angel, like a saint. He wondered what he should do with it. He had lived a quiet life, ignoring his own accomplishments. He didn't know how far he had run; he had no record of his personal best or how long it took him to complete a challenge, he had no medals. He hadn't felt like he had done enough to deserve those things or to deserve gratitude. He had done as much as he could to help people like the women he met on the path, but it was a drop in the ocean compared to what they needed.

He looked at the painting again, seeing the exact clarity with which the woman had painted him. It was from her, the woman from the path, the woman he had helped on that awful morning. It was how she remembered him. Above, swooping in like a superhero.

He took the picture to his living room and pulled a generic print off the wall. He hung the painting nervously, wondering if he should feel uncomfortable having his own eyes staring back at him. But he didn't. All he felt was pride. This moment that the woman had captured, above all of his medals and all of his races, was something he would display with pride. This was his best achievement. His first act of pure kindness.

The Young Girl

The young girl had been invited for a sleepover at her friend's house, and she couldn't be more excited. This would be her first since her parents' separation. She was nervous; what if she fell asleep before her host? What if she woke up earlier and was forced to lie on the cold, hard floor in her sleeping bag, waiting patiently until her friend woke up? What if they watched a scary movie and she had nightmares? What if her friend's creepy brother came in and started being strange?

A thousand thoughts ran through her head as she started to pack her overnight bag. The sleepover wasn't until the weekend, but she wanted to be prepared. Then she had a sudden, horrifying realisation. Her pyjamas were too small; not only that, but they were covered in a pattern of flying unicorns. Oh god, what if her friend saw those pyjamas and thought she was a baby? What if she mocked her at school and her new friend decided she wasn't cool enough to hang around with anymore? Panic started to rise within her body.

Her friend was definitely cool. She wore reasonably trendy clothes and spoke to the coolest boys. She had gone further with a boy than any other girl in their year and had an older boyfriend that her parents didn't know about. The friend was already talking about blow-jobs and wanking like they were everyday occurrences. She'd even booked herself in at the doctors for the pill so she'd be ready for when she and her boyfriend went "all the way".

The young girl was different; she didn't have a boy-friend and clammed up when young men in their school spoke to her. She was scared of men, a byproduct of having an alcohol-ridden, angry father.

She had only ever kissed one boy. Last week in the local park, during a game of spin the bottle. James King had breath that smelled like the Doritos he had eaten earlier and a huge spot on his chin. He had jammed his tongue into her mouth and nearly made her gag. Afterwards, her friends said how much he liked her and that they should start going out.

She wasn't sure.

~~The Wife~~, the Mother, the Woman, the Victim

The victim sat in her living room with her phone to her ear. It was the first Monday of the month, and she was making her regular phone call to the police officer friend for a case update. She already knew what they'd say. "No updates; we'll call you if there are." She wondered if it was time to put a stop to this ritual. But then again, she thought that every time she picked up the phone. No news is good news, people say. But not in this case; in this case, no news meant that a vile human being was still wandering the streets. Still eating fish and chips, still buying new socks and pants, and still potentially hurting other women.

The woman put the phone down after her brief conversation and sat staring blankly at the wall. Fifteen years was a long time to hide; it was a long time not to slip up and leave some other trace of evidence. The woman hoped and prayed that maybe he had seen the error of his ways and that her attack had been his first and last.

The Husband

He was now a father of two. Two boys. Born fifteen years apart but connected by his DNA and his blood. The baby was pronounced beautiful and handed over by the doctors to his exhausted wife. She didn't look any bit as glorious as his first wife had after giving birth.

He had expected her to snap back into shape like his first wife had as well, but she still looked pregnant. Her once firm, baby filled stomach was now a sagging wreck. She was breast feeding and milk was oozing out of her continuously, as if desperately trying to find its way into the child's mouth.

She'd had a second-degree tear and winced and moaned as she stood up and sat down. She screamed the first time she went to the toilet. She no longer wore nice clothes, staying in her pyjamas all day, even in front of the influx of visitors they received. She wore no makeup, but her pale face smiled as she proudly displayed their new born child to the guests.

Her parents were first. Two people who were clearly going to become overly indulgent grandparents. They arrived with arms full of flowers for his wife and a hamper of cotton onesies and teddies for the baby. He received no gift, something that irked him. After all, without his contribution this child wouldn't exist; he deserved some prize for his role.

His own son was second. He had stared into the Moses basket, spellbound by the tiny being within its wicker walls.

The Incident

His ex-wife had been next; she had brought a hand knitted blanket and some herbal tea for his wife. Upon seeing the blanket, his wife cried, pained tears flooding out of her eyes as she said thank you for the gift and began a huge apology for stealing the husband. His ex-wife had looked amused, and whilst holding his new wife's hand, she had said "that's alright sweetheart, if you need anything, just let me know". This had, of course, set his wife off with more floods, snot dribbling from her nose like a snail trail.

Not that it took a lot to set off the waterworks at the minute; his wife was always crying. He had taken to wondering if he should wear a wetsuit and snorkel around the house because of the quantity of her tears. There were great floods of them when the baby cried and when he wouldn't latch on. When she burned the toast or when her tea was forgotten, left undrunk and cold on the side. Enough tears to start their own small river, enough tears to bathe in. Enough to drown in.

The midwife had made some comments about "baby blues," but the husband knew what the real problem was. His wife was useless. What she needed was a good kick up the backside. She needed to get back to being her old sunny self, or he'd be forced to find his sunshine elsewhere.

Yet again.

The Watcher, the Waiter, the Hunter, the Husband

The watcher was expanding his talents. He didn't just watch anymore; he listened. He was outside his daughter's bedroom door when her friend was over, he was eavesdropping quietly on the other extension when his daughter used the house phone.

In the few short weeks since he had met the young girl, he knew almost everything about her. He knew that she hated maths, that she had only ever kissed one boy, and most importantly, he knew their plans for the sleepover at the weekend.

The Young girl

Her mother had saved the day by providing a new pair of pyjamas just hours before she went to her sleepover. Hurriedly brought from a local shop, they were light cotton covered in blue and red flowers. They had yellow piping on the edges and looked very grown-up. The perfect pair. The daughter didn't like to ask how much they cost. She knew money was tight and her mother was struggling, but still, she accepted the gift of the pyjamas, gave her mother a hug, and waited patiently for her friend to come and pick her up.

The girl's father pulled up outside the house and beeped his horn twice. Her mother had already left for work, so she locked the door and slipped the key into the inside pocket of her bag for safekeeping. Previously, when she had been to sleepovers, her mum had said to call her if she wanted to come home or if something happened and she felt uncomfortable. But this time she hadn't; the absent words had left a hole in their goodbye, and the young girl secretly wondered what she would do if she did want to come home. Her mother couldn't collect her. She was working, and the young girl had no one else to turn to. She knew her friend's parents wouldn't drive her back to an empty house at some god-awful time in the morning. Good parents didn't drive young girls back to empty homes.

The Watcher, the Waiter, the Hunter, the Husband

He watched as the young girl locked her door and left her house. She had a bag slung over her shoulder and seemed surprised when she got to the car and it was just him. He liked the way her face looked when she was surprised, her eyes widening and her mouth forming a small O. He explained to her that he'd left his wife at home cooking and that his daughter was blowing up the airbed.

He drove quickly, trying to keep his excitement to a minimum. The car was small, and he could smell the young girl. He would bet his next wage packet that she was wearing the same cherry lip balm that his daughter was obsessed with. He thought about kissing her cherry scented lips and wondered how they would taste. He tried to quell his excitement by turning up the radio and told himself it wouldn't be long until he found out.

The Young Girl

Her friend's mother had done them a buffet tea and was clearly pleased with her daughter's new choice of friend. Then both of the girls retreated to the bedroom and began the very serious task of gossiping and telling ghost stories. Her friend even told a horrible story about a rapist called the beast in the woods that she claimed was true.

Her friend had been planning this night for a while and was determined it would be epic, something they could brag about at school. She had already stolen a bottle of wine from her mum and dad's cupboard, and now both girls were taking sips directly from the bottle, giggling. The young girl didn't like the taste of wine and hated the idea of alcohol after watching her father slip under its grasp. But she didn't want to lose the only friend she had, so she kept sipping.

Neither of the girls had considered that the bottle of wine had been easy to find. Neither of them thought it was oddly convenient that the daughter's parents didn't come and check on them. Neither did they find it weird that the top had been unscrewed and screwed back on. Neither of them found the already dry taste slightly off or wondered why they were so drowsy after only half a bottle.

Neither of them considered anything; they just slept heavily.

The Watcher, the Waiter, the Hunter, the Husband

The house was silent. His son slept soundly in his bed, and his wife was already in theirs, snoring. In the soft pink glow of his daughter's bedroom, two girls slept side by side with half a bottle of wine balanced precariously on the table beside them.

The Rohypnol had been easier to get his hands on than he thought possible; a few words in a questionable man's ear could lead to a handful of tablets if the price was right. He had given his son and wife one each and helped them to bed, ignoring the confused looks in their dozy eyes. His wife had mumbled that it might be the flu and that she hoped they wouldn't make the young girl sick. His son had said nothing.

He stared at the two girls in the room and briefly considered having them both. No, he wasn't some sort of pervert; he wouldn't harm his daughter, but her friend was a different matter. She was irresistible.

He carried her to the living room, ready to begin his project.

The Young Girl

The young girl had the faint sensation of being moved. Her limbs felt heavy, and her head was fuggy. Every time she tried to open her eyes, the room swam in front of her. She couldn't be sure where she was. She knew she shouldn't have drunk the wine. She had seen her father pass out often enough and hoped nervously that she wouldn't embarrass herself.

Thoughts swam before her, the words her mother never said, never offering her escape, the face of her friend and the similar one of her brother. She drowsily wondered if it was his shadow she'd seen under the bathroom door while she changed.

Her thoughts swirled around her, enveloping her in chaos until, at last, she fell asleep. She wanted her mum.

The Young Girl, the Victim

The young girl awoke on a sagging air mattress. She could feel the hard floor beneath her bum. She also felt warm and sticky. She checked to see if her friend was still asleep and put a hand down her pyjamas. It came back faintly red. A watery red. The young girl deduced that she had started her period and went to the small bathroom to clean up. She hoped she hadn't stained the mattress.

She got dressed quickly and waited for her friend to awaken. Trying to ignore the throbbing coming from down below. Her mother said periods hurt, but the young girl hadn't had enough of them to know if this kind of hurt was normal; she definitely felt sorer than usual. She pushed her blood-stained pyjamas into her bag, thinking she'd have to wash them as soon as she got home so they wouldn't stain, and then her friend awoke. They went into the kitchen, where her friend's father was making pancakes. A huge smile was on his face.

As he flipped the pancakes and made silly faces out of them using fruits and berries, the young girl mused about what it must be like to have a father like this. A father who made pancakes on a Saturday morning with a smile on his face rather than one who woke up in a pool of his own vomit and a bad mood.

~~The Wife~~, the Mother, the Woman, the Victim

Her mother was sick. Well, if old age is a sickness at least. Hospital tests had shown that nothing was really wrong, but her body was slowing down. Nursing homes had been suggested, but her mother had scoffed. If she were dying, she would be doing it at home, in her bed, surrounded by her things, in the same place her husband had died. She was insistent.

The woman had gone to stay with her. Somebody was needed to take care of the day-to-day things, the washing, the cooking, and the cleaning. But mainly, her mother needed company. She was scared of death, scared of entering into the unknown alone. She still felt twenty, she still had adventures she wanted to take, and she had never seen the northern lights. She still had stories to tell. They had taken to sitting every evening in her mother's room, and the woman knitted while the old woman recounted her life chapter by chapter. Sometimes she missed bits, sometimes she jumped whole decades just to go back to one vital point.

The mother's son visited often. Trying to keep tears at bay while the old woman recounted her life. They all sat together, waiting.

The Young Girl, the Victim

School was awful again. She and her friend had fallen out. Her friend's brother had begun texting her, asking her out, and asking to kiss her, and the young girl hadn't known how to respond. In the end, she had given up and gone for ice cream with him.

They had a nice time, as it turns out he wasn't odd or creepy; he was just shy and incredibly lonely, like she had once been. Her friend had found out and hit the roof, saying that she had only used her for her brother. She had treated the young girl like a possession, getting jealous of her new friendship, and in the end, she had stopped all contact, and to make matters worse, she had made the other girls stop talking to her too. The boy had been expelled from school for fighting, and now, as if things couldn't get more horrible, she was getting fat.

One of the girls in her class had unkindly pointed it out after swimming, and now she was known as the fat girl. The lonely fat girl.

The Watcher, the Waiter, the Hunter, the Husband

The waiter took his annual pilgrimage to his mother's grave. It was located in a small town in which he had once committed a heinous crime. After he had placed flowers on his mother's grave, he would take a stroll down a woodland path, admiring the poppies that now bloomed next to the trees. Then he would go home, to the house he inhabited with his wife and children. Another place he had committed a crime.

He was old, and he was tired. The past few months had been filled with anxiety about the split condom. He had held his breath for the 72 hours it took for the drugs to leave his victim's body. Then he waited for the knock at the door of the young girl's mother.

It never came; the mother never visited, and slowly the young girl stopped visiting too. He was glad; the shine had left her now that he'd tasted her, and he was wondering what to do next. He was still struggling to find prostitutes. He'd been using the next town over, but now they were drying up, and he was bored again. His daughter had other friends, but he had known them since they were children. Every time he looked at them, he saw the faces of chubby toddlers. Even he couldn't go that far.

His son had been expelled for fighting and was now being tutored by a young woman. She was pretty in a certain way, but she had none of the magical spark he liked in his conquests. He had followed her a few times,

trying desperately to see if there was something underneath the surface that might pique his interest, but there
wasn't. But he was bored, so she might have to do.

The Young Girl, the Victim

Her body was flooded with pain. This wasn't an ordinary period. She had requested to go home from school, and with one look at her sweating face, the school secretary had packed her off. She probably thought she was contagious and was trying to think of the other students in the school. Nobody wanted a sickness bug going around. But more than likely, the receptionist didn't want the responsibility of scrubbing vomit off the carpet or dealing with the smell of sick for the next few days.

She had struggled to get home, having to grip the sides of walls to keep herself upright. Now she was in the small house she and her mother rented, rocking on all floors in the middle of the bathroom, hoping to God that she wouldn't die.

Her mother was working; she'd been pulling extra shifts trying to find enough money for Christmas. She knew she couldn't call her, but she felt like fire was trying to eat her from the inside.

She rang her mother's phone, and it was answered immediately. She simply spoke two words. "Help me".

The Watcher, the Waiter, the Hunter, the Husband

Whilst the young girl was squirming in pain on her bathroom floor, the hunter spent his evening sitting in a pub fifty miles away. He was waiting for one of the girls to get so drunk that he could take them outside and release some of his carnal lust.

At last, he found his target, a young woman. As he took her outside and began to try to remove her clothes, a rowdy group of rugby lads heard her scream. They beat him till he was black and blue, spitting on him and threatening to phone the police.

He ran and threw his wallet into a bush.

When he explained the bruises to his wife, he said he had been mugged.

The Young Girl, the Victim, the Mother

The young girl tried to comprehend what had happened over the last few months. It had started in the bathroom, with her sobbing on the floor, mentally begging her mother to be quicker, to get there sooner, and to help her. Her mother's shocked face as she entered the room, and their joint surprise when a baby slid from between her legs onto her dressing gown.

A baby. From a virgin.

They had both cried, arms wrapped around each other in astonishment. For a few moments, the baby lay on the floor, as if both women were afraid to touch it. As if holding it would make it real and solid. Then her mother had come to her senses, wrapped it in the dressing gown, and held it close to her body for warmth, rocking back and forth. An ambulance had been called, a man and a woman paramedic who had clearly seen their fair share of unexpected pregnancies and just nodded sympathetically when she said she hadn't had sex. They didn't believe her; they thought she was trying to cover up her sexual activity in front of her mother. But she wasn't lying.

A doctor in the hospital had been amazed that she had given birth alone, at home, without even realising it. Her father had been notified and had arrived at the hospital looking clean and alert for once, holding a bunch of flowers in his hand as he tried to tactfully ask his daughter what had happened. Yet again, the young girl reiterated that she was a virgin. A nurse came in, clearly under the instruction of her parents, and told her that you could get pregnant with just a drop of semen, even if it was on a finger. Yet again, the young girl defended herself, eventually screaming that she had only ever kissed one boy.

The baby, a girl had come home with her. She didn't want it, but her mother had insisted. The young girl didn't know what to do; she was young, and she had no idea where this thing had come from. At her mother's insistence, she fed it bottles and changed its nappies, all the time wondering if it could be real. It couldn't be, surely. You had to have sex to have a baby. She'd sat through enough biology lessons to know that traditionally, a penis had to be inserted into a vagina; to use schoolyard talk, you had to "do it". She started to wonder if God was real and if all the jokes about the virgin mother being a whore who told good stories were wrong. After all, she was a virgin mother.

She began pretending to be asleep so her mother would care for the child. The young girl didn't want to touch it; it was cursed. Her father moved in, sleeping on the sofa, his long legs hanging over the arm. He was finally sober.

The school wondered where she was, and her mother went in to explain. She asked the teachers for information, for their own personal knowledge. The teachers all replied the same; the young girl was quiet. They had never seen her with any boys.

The mother called the girl's old friend and asked her. She was told honestly that the only boy the young girl had been on a date with was her brother. She went home and began to accuse her daughter.

As her mother stood screaming at her to tell the truth, the girl cracked and screamed back. She didn't know where the baby was from; she didn't know how it got there. She had never had sex. Her father, who had been a bystander during the exchange, looked into his daughter's eyes and saw only the truth. He sent the young girl to bed and sat at the kitchen table with his estranged wife.

He explained to her that he knew lies and that they had been his bread and butter while he drank his life away. He told his wife that this couldn't be a lie and sat at the kitchen table it became apparent to both of the young girl's parents that things were darker than they seemed.

The young girl begged every day for the baby to be adopted, to be taken to a place where she didn't have to look at it, didn't have to touch it, but her mother refused. The baby was their only link to finding out the truth. They needed the baby.

The young girl watched as her parents sat every night trying to piece together what had happened in the young girl's life nine months previously. They phoned relatives who might remember; they looked at the calendar, which held only a record of the mother's work shifts and they checked receipts. It was the receipts that gave them their first clue. Brand new pyjamas, trimmed with yellow piping, brought for the young girl's first sleepover with her new friend. Where coincidentally a boy she had previously had a date with also slept.

The Watcher, the Waiter, the Hunter

The police were at the door. His blood was running cold. Was this it? Had he been found out? He wondered what they knew. Was it the young woman from the path? Was it the young girl? Was it the one from the pub? Surely it couldn't be the busty woman from his old job?

He hoped it wasn't the one from the pub. She hadn't deserved his attention anyway, and he hadn't even finished. He was relieved to find they wanted to speak to his son and terrified when they said he was being questioned in relation to a rape.

The Young Girl, the Victim, the Mother

Her mother was a woman possessed. She had found the culprit; she had found the father of the young girl's baby, and DNA would prove it.

DNA, however, did not find that the creepy young man was the father's child. It only showed that they were related. It had taken the mother of the young girl longer than she would have liked to piece together what that meant.

It took the young girl only seconds. As she looked at the small child in the Moses basket, she immediately saw something that she had been ignoring. Her child looked exactly like her best friend in the countless baby photos that were scattered around her house.

She remembered the night of the sleepover. How the wine had made her feel funny, how a shadow had stood outside the door as she changed, not the shadow of a boy, the shadow of a man. She thought about how her friend's father had picked her up and how he had guided her up the path to their home with his hand on the small of her back. She thought about how she had felt in the morning, sticky and sore.

She thought past the sleepover, to the days when the smell of frying bacon had made her feel sick, to the irregular periods she had, her boobs not fully formed but feeling sore in their cotton cups.

The Incident

She thought to her bloated stomach, to the girls in the changing room mocking her weight, calling her a whale, and asking her if she'd seen Jonah lately.

Then, as her mother spoke to the police for what felt like the hundredth time, she vomited all over the floor.

~~The Wife~~, the Mother, the Woman, the Victim

Her mother was clinging onto her life while the woman's lay forgotten. She hadn't visited her own home in months and hadn't picked up the phone to inquire about her case. She wasn't obsessed with the location of the man who hurt her.

She was exhausted. Every night was a struggle, wondering if this would be the day she woke up without a mother, not daring to sleep in case she missed the vital moment. The very second her mother faded, the last goodbye. Every day she wondered if today would be the day that she became the head of her small family. The day she became an orphan.

Her son had noticed her tiredness and ordered her home for the night. He insisted that his grandmother wouldn't die without a full house of mourning visitors. An audience to witness her final curtain call. Her mother had agreed.

She went back to her home and was momentarily surprised by how unfamiliar it felt. She'd left the heating on, so the tape that held pictures and sketches to the wall had curled and shrivelled, letting patches of colour drop and exposing the white walls beneath.

There was milk in the fridge that had created its own eco system, dirty washing that would have to be thrown away, and dust settled on every surface.

And the light was blinking incessantly on the answering machine.

The Watcher, the Waiter, the Hunter, the Husband

Time was up.

The Police Officer, The Mother

The police officer stared at the case file in her hands. This file had dogged her career for the past fifteen years. It was a folder of failures. A folder of very little evidence for a case no one had thought would be solved. This file had been in her home. She had studied it so often that she knew the words by heart. She knew the victim's phone number better than her own. The back page bore a red crayon line from her own son. It was finally over; she finally had a conclusion. She finished typing her notes and added them to the file.

Then she opened the filing cabinet, staring at the countless other folders of cases that would probably never be solved, and said a prayer for the people they contained.

~~The Wife~~, the Mother, the Woman, the Victim

As she sat in the police station office, she felt her head reeling. An information overload. He had been caught. He had raped at least one other woman, not even a woman, a young girl. A young girl the same age as his daughter. He had a daughter, and he had a family. That beast of a man had made a life for himself after what he had done. The young girl he had raped had had a child, and DNA had proved him to be the father. Vomit churned again in her stomach. The police officer recognised the reaction and offered her a waste paper basket.

As she was sick, words swam around her head. Date rape, teenage pregnancy, second victim. The police officer walked over "put your head between your knees." The victim obeyed, and the room stopped spinning.

He had been caught; even at this very moment, he was behind bars. He had confessed to two crimes, the one he had just committed with an underage girl and the one he had committed fifteen years previously with herself. They had even found the underwear she had worn that hideous day, concealed in a safe in his house. The DNA was a perfect match. The hunter's wife had opened the safe for the visiting police officers. Had she known?

She felt relieved and sad at the same time. This was how her story came to a close; this is how that chapter of her life ended. With a young girls now torn apart. For her to find closure, a young girl would have to start

237

her own rebirth. She felt guilty, and for the first time since the incident, she wished she had been raped again. She would have that pig lay his hands on her a thousand more times if it meant saving the young girl that she didn't know but to whom she was so deeply connected.

She was filled with questions; she was made entirely of queries that needed to be resolved. Why did he rape her? Why did he rape the young girl? How long would he be jailed for? Was the young girl okay? Was she keeping her baby? Her chest contracted with each question and each new train of thought.

The police officer could not answer any questions. The cases, plural now, hadn't even been put before a judge yet. At the moment, he was quite simply awaiting trial in prison. He could get fifteen to twenty years. Fifteen years as a minimum; the woman had already served that time for his crime. She had lived it every day whilst he went off and got married, had children, and built a life. While he lived as an innocent, free to wander the world, she had been trapped by a prison of her own design. Walls built high to protect herself from the world outside. Fifteen years of purgatory where she had avoided letting people get any closer than arm's length. Fifteen years was younger than the last girl he hurt. It was ridiculous. It made her angry; fury began to circulate her veins, and cold, hard anger replaced the sickness in her stomach.

The woman went home to her expectant son and mother. They saw her tears and her rage and knew what had happened instantly. Together, they sat on the bed the old woman was dying in and cried. Trying to work out why this should mean the end for them and the beginning for others.

The Young Girl, the Victim, the Mother

The young girl had a spread of adoption leaflets fanned out in front of her on the kitchen table. Her mother had finally agreed. The leaflets had been left by a social worker and explained the options, open, closed. Did she want updates? Did she want contact?

She was doing better now. She felt a good sense of clarity that what had happened had finally been resolved. She still felt sick inside at the thought of what that man had done to her whilst she slumbered unawares, but she was getting counselling, and she felt relieved that she had no memory of what had happened to her. After the adoption she would have a fresh start.

She looked at the baby in the basket and once again apologised. She held the little girl's chubby fingers and reassured her that she would find the best, most loving parents she could. She wondered if she would have kept her if she had known, or if she would have snuck off to have an abortion.

She knew in her head that she couldn't raise her, not after the way she had been brought into the world, but she had to admit the baby had certain endearing qualities. As she had grown, she looked less like the friend she had once had and more like the young girl. She'd even taken the time to name her after they had all called her baby for months, but the adoption service had informed her that the new parents may wish to change the name, and she was okay with that.

The Incident

The adoption lady was going to call her today with some options and to talk everything over. Very soon, this baby girl would have a whole new life ahead of her that wouldn't be clouded by the way in which she had begun.

~~The Watcher, the Waiter, the Hunter, the Husband,~~ the Prisoner

Everything had been stripped from him; he wasn't a name anymore he was a number. He was a property of the government, of her majesty. They had taken his things, his watch, and his wallet. Even his shoes. He had been stripped and searched; they had checked him for hidden items. He felt violated. He had been forced to squat over a mirror.

He sat in his cell now. He found he didn't mix well with the other prisoners. As it turns out, even the most hardened murderers and drug dealers draw the line at child rape. He had been advised by a guard to stay in his room until they could move him to another prison. A place that didn't know his crime. Where they could fabricate a lie for his incarceration. But it was difficult as other inmates shouted things into his cell. They threatened him through concrete walls and pissed on him in the showers.

He just had to wait until his verdict, and then he could ask to be transferred. They did that sometimes, the government didn't want too many prisoners killing each other; it spoiled the rehabilitation angle they were selling.

He continued to sit in his cell, running over what the police did and didn't know in his mind. He needed to keep his story straight; he couldn't give anything else away. They knew about the young woman, but they didn't know about the dog or his mother. They knew about the young girl, but they didn't know about the woman from the bar or that he had drugged his wife and kids; realistically, he was doing quite well. He'd gotten away with a lot, and the sentence for rape was a lot less than the one for murder. Good behaviour might even see him free before he was an old man. His body might hang on for long enough for him to taste a woman again.

In fact, the watcher, the waiter, the hunter was so absorbed in his own thoughts he didn't notice a prison guard unlocking his cell, a fist full of money stuffed in his pocket, nor did he notice the four huge Russians enter it.

In fact, he didn't notice anything out of the ordinary until he felt two strong hands around his throat, choking the life out of him. As his eyes began to cloud over, he felt one of the men whisper in his ear.

The Mother, the Grandmother, the Wife, ~~the Mother in Law~~

The old woman lay in the bed she would die in with a phone in her hand. It was a cheap, tacky thing, nothing like the mini computers young people used today. Her daughter had fallen asleep in the chair by the side of the bed, and her grandson was curled up at the end like a cat.

Her grandson had been wrong; she didn't need an audience to die, she just needed justice. She and her late husband had many secrets, and they had made many promises. He was a quiet man, so when he did choose to speak, it gave his words a certain weight and gravity. Fifteen years ago, he had said his heaviest words yet "I want him dead".

Her husband was not one for grand dramatics as she and her daughter were; he was a man of his word, and she knew he was serious. She noticed him peacefully going about his business and knew he was planning something. Her husband was a man of many acquaintances, a man who was owed many favours. He knew the right people to ask and the right ways to plan, and ever the good wife, she was at his right hand, ready to use her words to convey his message.

Sadly, he had died too soon to see his plan in action, but not before making his wife promise that she would continue and that she would see their work finished. That if she had the opportunity, if she was sure, if there was no doubt, she would carry out the plan.

The old woman sat smugly in bed. It wasn't hard to plan a murder; you just had to know the right people and have the right sort of money. She and her husband had been thrifty their entire marriage, treating every penny like a prisoner and every pound as a hostage. Dmitri, a Russian gangster of sorts, had been acquired some years ago and put under an extended contract. Much to his amusement, he had been met in a quaint coffee shop by an old couple who wished to avenge their daughter's rape. They wanted the rapist dead. They were willing to pay. The old woman smiled, remembering the shock on the burly mobster's face as they explained what they wanted, information and, ideally, a body, all while she filled up his plate with scones and clotted cream.

Dmitri had no luck finding information but stayed in touch via the phone the old woman had in her hand. If they needed him, all they had to do was call. The old woman had been concerned that they may never find out who the attacker was. But good things come to those who wait, and she had fifteen years of patience on her side. She had been worried that now that he was in prison, it might make him untouchable, but Dmitri said it actually made it easier. An animal caught in a trap was the expression he used. He had plenty of friends inside, people who would be happy to have a large sum of money deposited into their wives bank accounts or a kilo of drugs smuggled into the prison for them to sell in exchange for one small job.

A small job. She liked the way Dmitri described it. Like killing that vile man was no bigger than squashing a spider. Like disposing of him would be no more effort than taking a wheelie bin full of rubbish onto the curb for collection.

The old woman looked at the message on the phone screen once more. It confirmed that the task had been done. She removed the SIM card from the back of the phone and snapped it between her fingers, the force made her bones hurt, but she was weary anyway. She threw the shards over her shoulder like salt. Hoping to keep evil spirits from ever entering their lives once more. The most basic form of witchcraft, a mother's hope.

Then she stuffed the phone beneath the mound of blankets that kept her old, cold bones warm. Chances were that when her daughter was ready, she would just pick up the pile and throw them into the washing machine. The phone would be destroyed. She spread her hands over the blankets she had knitted for her husband, a fortress against death.

She thought about her grandson, about how he was a kind and solid man, she thought about her ex-son in law, about how he hated her and as the darkness began to take her, she thought about her beautiful daughter, the woman who had found that there was something lower than rock bottom and had slowly but surely built herself back up and adjusted the habits of her life.

She thought of her beloved husband and how they would be together soon, reunited at last. She thought of the life they had shared and the justice they had served together. As the air began to leave her lungs for the last time, her daughter slept soundly in the chair, and her grandson slumbered at the end of the bed.

The Incident

As the old woman died, the hunter's lifeless body was being carried to the icy prison mortuary. The last words he had ever heard were a message from the old woman, from the mother of his victim.

"Rot in hell, motherfucker."

Not the End

Life is a continual spiral of events, a flowing line that links one life to another, one event to the next. There is never an end. There are only fresh new beginnings for those who are willing to take them.

The Incident

Acknowledgements

This book had been in my head for quite a while. It formed itself on the long walk me and my son had to school every morning. Luckily, in 2021, we all found ourselves at the mercy of COVID lockdown, and I found myself without an excuse for not having enough time to write it.

I would like to thank my Mum Carol and Sister Netty for being my first readers; without their encouragement and cheerleading, I never would have carried on.

I'd like to thank my Brother-in-Law Keith for making it one of the only books he has ever read and telling me that was a good enough reason to get it put into print.

I'd like to thank Auntie Debbie for the countless hours she spent proofreading my horrendous spelling mistakes and grammar. We've come a long way since you used to listen to me read in primary school.

The Incident

I'd like to thank my Dad Brian for working so bloody hard the entire time I was growing up and telling me constantly that if I wanted to do something, I should trust my gut and go for it.

Also, my Brother Stuart, who told me to stop talking about it and just finish it. As always, your bluntness really hit the nail on the head.

A special thanks to my partner John, who has never read this and probably never will. You are my safe place. Thank you for putting up with the constant nights of typing, the screaming at the printer, and the searching for words.

And finally, I'd like to thank my Son Marcus. Everything I have done and everything I will do has been for you, and even though in hindsight some of those things weren't for the best, they were always for you. You are my light.

Disclaimer:

The places, incidents, and people in this book have never happened and are a work of my imagination. If you see similarities to true events, it is purely coincidental.

However, if you are reading the book and finding similarities between yourself and some of the "asshole" characters, I suggest you take a long, hard look at your life and re-evaluate things.

My mother would also like to clarify that although the personality of the victim's mother was inspired by her, she is far more fabulous and bears absolutely no resemblance to "an old film star who had fallen from grace and was desperate for attention."

Printed in Great Britain
by Amazon

30760063R00148